MW01287275

THE LEMON

ALSO FROM CITY LIGHTS

A HUNDRED CAMELS IN THE COURTYARD
by Paul Bowles

M'HASHISH
by Mohammed Mrabet, taped and translated by Paul Bowles

THE OBLIVION SEEKERS
by Isabelle Eberhardt, translated by Paul Bowles

THE BEGGAR'S KNIFE
by Rodrigo Rey Rosa, translated by Paul Bowles

LOVE WITH A FEW HAIRS
by Mohammed Mrabet, taped and translated by Paul Bowles

THE LEMON

Mohammed Mrabet

Translated from the Moghreb
and edited in collaboration with
Mohammed Mrabet

by PAUL BOWLES

City Lights Books
San Francisco

Cover: detail from a drawing by Mohammed Mrabet

City Lights acknowledges with thanks:
Ned Leavitt and Flora Day

Library of Congress Cataloging-in-Publication Data

Mrabet, Mohammed, 1940-
  The lemon.

  I. Bowles, Paul, 1910-   . II. Title.
PJ7850.R3L4 1986   892'.736   85-29148
ISBN 0-87286-181-3 (pbk.)

CITY LIGHTS BOOKS are edited by Lawrence Ferlinghetti
& Nancy J. Peters and published at the City Lights Bookstore,
261 Columbus Avenue, San Francisco, California 94133.

THE LEMON

1

Across the street from the house where Abdeslam lived there was a mosque. Here the boys chanted their lessons all day. When Abdeslam was six years old his father told him it was time for him too to go and study the Koran with the others.

The first day his father went with him and gave some money to the fqih. Look after him. Make him learn, he said, and then he went away.

Abdeslam sat down facing the fqih. He did not know what was going to happen, but he thought the fqih would probably give him a hanasha, a board to write on. Instead of that, he made him sit with the other boys and sing the letters of the alphabet after him : *a-lif, el-ba, et-tsa,* and so on. They did this all day for many days, Abdeslam and the others, singing the letters after the fqih. Then one morning the fqih told them : Today I'm going to pass out hanashas, so you can learn to write and read the letters faster.

Abdeslam was delighted. He and the boys rocked

back and forth and pounded their hanashas while they recited the letters. When he told his father about it, he went out and bought him a fine board of cedar-wood from Moulay Brahim, so he would always have something to hit while he sang the letters. His father told him that this way the letters would go straight into his head and stay there. Some of the other boys brought hanashas from home, too, made of apple- or olive-wood, but they did not smell as good as Abdeslam's.

The fqih began to teach the boys the beginning of the Koran. In two years' time Abdeslam already had reached the *Baqra Seghira.* His father went to the mosque and said to the fqih: I hear my son has got to the *Baqra Seghira.* Is that true?

Yes, said the fqih. It is true, thanks to Allah.

Two years is very little time in which to learn so much of the Koran. Abdeslam had learned fast because his father's brother, who lived in the house with his family and could read the Koran very well, had taken him into his room each day when he got home from school and taught him more.

Abdeslam's father thanked the fqih. Then he and his brother went to the cattle-souq and bought a young bull. They led it home and killed it, and invited thirty tolba to come and recite the Koran. The tolba were all young men who knew it perfectly and were used to chanting it together. It was late at night when they finished. Then Abdeslam's mother and sisters served them the flesh of the bull in a couscous.

Abdeslam enjoyed his life. There was the world outside, with trees and houses and places to play, and the world of words and letters in the mosque. He felt that he was learning more every day.

It was a year or so later when his father met him at the

door as he came home from school one day, and said to him : You' fqih tells me you know the whole first part of the Book, and can read it and write it. That's good. Now you're going to go to school.

Abdeslam did not want this. He knew it was a harder kind of work. Why can't I stay at the mosque? he said. I want to be a fqih.

You've got to learn arithmetic and French and all sorts of things. You don't know anything yet. Later you can be a fqih.

But Baba, I like it at the mosque. I won't understand anything at the school. I want to learn more of the Koran.

School, said his father.

Abdeslam sighed.

2

One day a few months later Abdeslam's father took him to the school. He spoke a while with the principal, and then he left Abdeslam alone with him.

Come, said the man, and he led Abdeslam down a corridor into a room where the teacher was a Frenchwoman.

Madame Titagaux, this boy will be in your class, he told her. He doesn't understand any French at all. Only Arabic. You'll have to help him a little.

Oui, monsieur le Directeur.

After a while she sat down with Abdeslam and began to explain things to him. She was patient and kind with him. Each day she would guide his hand, and he would write the letters one by one. She showed him how to write new words, and he learned very easily. After three months he could write whatever she asked him to write.

Our teacher is wonderful, he told his father. She's taught me French. I've learned how to read and write it, and I can speak a little, too.

Hamdoul'lah! said his father. And keep away from

those boys outside in the street. I don't want to see you playing with them. The next thing you'll be talking like them.

At the end of his second year with Madame Titagaux, Abdeslam had second place in his French class. But before the third year was finished, Madame Titagaux was called back to France. The afternoon before she left she had all the boys go out into the playground under the cypress trees, and there she told them that she was going away and that she was very sorry to be leaving them. They all said : *Bon voyage, madame.*

She let the other boys go home, but she kept Abdeslam with her, and asked him to carry her brief-case out to the car for her. Then she drove him to his house, and when he got out she gave him some books and some pens and pencils, and kissed him good-bye.

The next morning the boys sat in the classroom waiting. When the teacher came in the pupils all stood up. He was tall and thin, with very light-coloured hair, and he wore a black suit and glasses. He walked the way a woman walks. He smiled at the boys and said : *Bonjour, mes enfants.*

They all said : *Bonjour, monsieur.*

You may be seated, he told them. He had a cane, and he put it across his knees. He said : *Vous êtes tous très gentils.* I hope you will always be just like this. Quiet. Now, Madame Titagaux has gone away and I am here. I hope you will like me just as much as you did her.

At the end of each sentence he shut his mouth very quickly. He got up, took a piece of chalk, and began to write on the blackboard. Then he drew lines and said : *Ça, c'est un chat.* And the boys had to say : *Oui, ça, c'est un chat.* He erased the lines and wrote some more, and drew some more lines. *Ça, c'est un chien.* And the boys had to say the words after him. Madame Titagaux had never done that. Abdeslam could not understand what the new teacher was doing, and he did not believe that the man was a real teacher. He thought it more likely that he was a friend of someone important in the government.

At recess he heard the other boys saying: That's not a man. That's a woman. Everything he does is like a woman. Even when he's just walking he dances.

Monsieur Jacques would take the chalk and write on the blackboard. When he had written several lines of words he would say: Look well at these words and learn them by heart. Then he would erase all the words and say: Now, write. Each day he would write longer sentences, until it became impossible to remember them all.

One day Abdeslam went to the principal's office.

What's the matter, Abdeslam?

That new teacher.

What about him?

He writes a lot of words on the blackboard and then rubs them out, and says we have to write them afterwards. But nobody can get even the first line. We haven't got machines inside our heads.

The principal told Abdeslam to go to his classroom. But the next day when Monsieur Jacques came in to give the French lesson he cried: Abdeslam!

Oui, monsieur.

Une autre fois tu ne feras pas comme ça! Comme tu es méchant!

Abdeslam began to whisper with Hamidou. He's no teacher, he was saying. He comes in and talks like a woman, and snaps his mouth shut like a turtle. He's nothing.

While he was whispering, Monsieur Jacques called his name

Oui, monsieur.

Come up here.

When Abdeslam got to the big desk, Monsieur Jacques stood up. Kneel down, now, he told him. Right at my feet.

Why, monsieur?

Get down on your knees!

I can't do that for you, monsieur, said Abdeslam. You're a Nazarene and I'm a Moslem. How can I kneel in front of you? I don't do that even for my father. When I get home all I do is kiss his hand.

A genoux! screamed Monsieur Jacques.

Non!

When Monsieur Jacques heard that, he drew back his arm and slapped Abdeslam's cheek very hard. Abdeslam sprang upwards and threw himself at Monsieur Jacques with such force that he fell backwards against a step-ladder behind him and lost his balance. Before he could rise to his feet again, Abdeslam ran out of the room. He went out of the school, down the steps, through the streets, to his house.

His father was at home. When he saw Abdeslam he jumped up. What are you doing here at this hour? he cried.

I had a fight with the French teacher. I won't go back to school. Ever!

His father hit him twice with the back of his hand, and Abdeslam fell down. His head struck the edge of a shelf, and it hurt. He started to cry.

Now get out of here and don't come back! shouted his father, I don't know you. You're not my son and I'm not your father. I don't want to see you anywhere in this neighbourhood. Get up! Now go!

Abdeslam stood looking at his father. He had stopped crying. One of his father's wives began to sob. Why throw him out into the street? she said. Your own son?

Keep out of this, he told her.

Abdeslam picked up one small book off the floor and went out. He walked in the streets for a while. Soon he met a group of boys he knew, sitting on the ground by a wall. He sat down with them. One of them pulled out a cigarette and offered it to him.

No thanks, he said.

You don't want it? What's the matter with you?

Nothing, he said. I've got to go now.

3

In Boubana there was a friend of his father's who he thought might give him a place to sleep that night. He set out across the hillside to Boubana. As he got down to the bottom of the valley at Oued Bahrein it began to rain a little. There was a house standing alone in a field not far from the road, with an open garage next to it. He walked quickly into the garage and decided that this would be a good place to spend the night. He sat down and waited for dark to come, and then he fell asleep.

When he awoke in the morning the sun was shining. He got up, and in spite of what his father had said, went back to his own neighbourhood. He was sure that even if his father should see him, he would be able to get away from him. He spent the day playing in the streets and orchards with his friends, and they brought him things to eat from their houses.

It got late, and he walked back out to the country to sleep again in the garage. On the way, it began to rain again, the same as the day before. It was dusk when he got to Oued Bahrein, and he found that someone had shut the garage door. He turned and began to walk up the hill towards the cemetery, thinking : There must be some place to sleep.

He decided to go again to his own neighbourhood. The rain was falling harder. At the entrance to El Mraier there was a house with many windows. It belonged to Juan Rico. Next door was another house, with a big doorway. Abdeslam went and stood underneath it, looking out at the rain. Everything was wet. He could not sit down. Finally he fell asleep and slumped against the door.

Early in the morning people began to go past on their way to work. Someone shook him. He opened his eyes. A man was bending over him.

What are you doing here, son?

Sleeping.

This is no place to sleep. Haven't you got a family?

Abdeslam did not answer.

Are you hungry? Come with me.

No, sidi, I'm all right, said Abdeslam. I can look out for myself.

The man put his hand into his pocket, took out two rials, and made him take them. Abdeslam started to walk. He went all the way into the Medina and sat down in a small restaurant there.

What will it be?

A bowl of harira.

The man served him the soup. Abdeslam asked for an extra order of sminn. When he had finished his harira he got up. How much? he said.

That's all right. It's from me.

Abdeslam thanked the man and walked down the street to the terrace of a café. He ordered a glass of tea, but before it came he went next door and bought some pastries to eat with his tea. He sat a while eating, drinking and looking at the people, and then he left. The rain had nearly stopped. He went up the hill thinking he would go and see the other boys in his quarter.

He found his friends in the ruined shed where they always met. They were playing cards and smoking. He sat with them, but he did not feel the same with them as he had before. When they left the shed they were all going home to their families, and he had nowhere to go. They gave him a little bread.

The rain stopped in the afternoon. When the other boys went home, Abdeslam walked into the country to a place where there were many eucalyptus trees. He felt a little sick, so he lay down on the ground under the trees. Soon it grew dark and began to rain again, but he had fallen asleep and knew nothing about it. The rain went on falling. When it had wet him a little, he woke up. One side of him was wet. The other side was still dry, and he was afraid to turn over or move, for fear of getting the other side wet. So he stayed in the same position, lying just as he was. As daybreak came the rain grew very light, so that it was almost like a mist.

Abdeslam got up and felt in his pocket. The little book he had brought with him was dry. He started back to his own quarter. There was a baker who had an oven in a side-street, and he decided to go and see him.

The baker stood in the doorway. Good morning, Abdeslam said to him. He went inside and saw that the fire was lit. Then he took off his clothes and dried them in front of it. When he was dressed, the man gave him some bread and a cup of coffee. When he pulled out a pack of cigarettes, he held it out to Abdeslam. Do you want one?

All right, said Abdeslam. He lighted the cigarette and

began to smoke it. He was glad he had come to see the baker.

Abdeslam, the man said. You're too young to smoke. You're still very small. Why don't you listen to your father and do what he wants you to?

How do you know about it?

We all know about it, the baker told him. It's not a secret. And here you are. You know how to read and write. You have a great future ahead of you. Why don't you go back to school and study? Think how happy your whole family would be. If you stay in the street like this, you'll be smoking cigarettes all day long, one after the other, and then you'll begin to drink. And the next thing you'll be going around with thieves and whores. You'll get into fights, and some day somebody'll kill you. How old are you? Ten? You've still got a lot of studying to do before you're a man.

I'm twelve, Abdeslam told him. Then he said: Yes, you're right, Si Mohammed, except that you don't understand.

You know what you want, son, said the baker. I feel sorry for you.

I've got to go now, said Abdeslam. Thanks. I'm all dry. Good luck with the oven.

He went down to the city and walked through the souks for an hour or so. At five o'clock he went to look at the pictures on the wall of the entrance of the Cinema Capitol. There were many people going in. Some boys from his neighbourhood came past. Each one gave a little, and they bought him a ticket. They all sat together and watched a film of Gary Cooper. Before it was over Abdeslam got up and whispered to his friends that he was going to the lavatory. Instead, he went out into the street.

The weather had turned very cold. He climbed the hill

and went out to his neighbourhood. Here he walked only in the alleys. His father's house was on a corner of the principal street, and he was afraid of meeting him. He was very hungry, but he kept walking, up and down the alleys. After a while he felt dizzy. He sat down beside the entrance door to a house, to wait until he was a little better. Then he realized that the house belonged to a Spaniard whom he knew.

Soon the door opened and a man came out. It was Paco.

Abdeslam! What are you doing here?

Just sitting.

You're not going home tonight, you mean?

That's right.

Why not?

My father threw me out.

But why?

For nothing. Because I won't go to school.

Come inside with me, Paco told him. Come in.

Abdeslam did not want to go into Paco's house, but Paco pulled him up and made him walk in. Then he shut the door. Mercedes, Paco's wife, was sitting there in a bathrobe. She got up when they entered. A few minutes later she went into the kitchen and prepared some food for Abdeslam.

While he was eating, Paco poured him a glass of wine. Here, he said. This will warm you up and make you feel good.

Nó, grácias.

Why not? Wine is good with food.

I'm a Moslem.

When he had finished eating, Abdeslam sat looking around the room. He had never been in a Nazarene house before. Mercedes was sitting in a big chair with her hands folded in her lap. The little boy and girl sat on the couch

17

playing. There was a big bed in the corner for Paco and Mercedes, and a small bed beside it for the children. Over the wardrobe was a picture of Paco and Mercedes the day they were married, another with the children, and a third one of Jesus Christ.

Soon Paco took him into the other room. It was small, but it had a bed in it, and many empty milk-pails. The walls were hung with cowbells.

This is where you're going to sleep, Paco told him. Mercedes came in with some sheets and a blanket, and Paco went and got him an old pair of pyjamas. After he had got into bed, Mercedes came and kissed him on the forehead.

Thank you, said Abdeslam.

Sleep well, she said. And until tomorrow.

She blew out the lamp. Then she went away and shut the door.

Abdeslam closed his eyes. When he opened them it was morning and Mercedes was standing by his bed. Come and have breakfast, she said.

4

In this way Abdeslam started a new life, hiding in the Nazarenes' house. They did not ask him to work, but he carried things for them, ran errands, and learned to milk the goats and cows. They gave him food and bought him clothes, and even said they would pay him for each month he had been with them, when the time came that he was ready to leave them.

Sometimes they would get up at five in the morning, and when Abdeslam went into the kitchen he would find Mercedes already there in her bathrobe, making coffee. Then while it was still dark they would go and milk the cows and some of the goats.

Abdeslam spent a good deal of time sitting in the house, reading the little book about Haroun er Rachid that he had brought with him from home. He read it all the way through, and soon he read it again. Mercedes would come and try to interest him in something else. He did not want to tell her that he could not go out and play with his friends, that this was why he stayed in the house reading.

He was afraid that if the other boys saw him they would find out where he was living, and one of them might tell his father.

At the end of the afternoon each day Abdeslam would go out and open the gates to let the goatherds in with the goats. Then he would shut each goat into its stall. When they were all inside he would take them raw beans and barley.

There was a story in his book that he liked more than the rest. It told how Haroun er Rachid used to go out of his palace at night, dressed like anyone else, and sit in cafés talking to the people. He imagined himself doing the same thing. Each night he would meet new people who would tell him their adventures, and he would learn about the world. He began to think about this during the day when he was working with Paco, and at night when he was going to sleep. Finally he was thinking about it nearly all the time. And he often wished he were not living in this neighbourhood and in this house with Paco and Mercedes, where he could not even go into the street for fear of his father. When he rode on the donkey into the city with Paco he would look down the narrow alleys of the Medina and think how much he would like to walk along one of them and disappear. Then his own adventures would start. He would have his own life. He decided he would have to tell Paco that he could not live there any longer.

One evening after dinner while they sat at the table, he began to talk, and to thank Paco and Mercedes for all the things they had done for him. But Paco interrupted him.

Abdeslam, when you're alone thinking, what do you think about? he wanted to know.

It would be better if I didn't tell you.

No, Abdeslam! Mercedes said, laughing. You've got to tell us.

I think about all the awful things that are going to happen to me. They're still far away, but they're coming closer. I can see them all happening in front of my eyes right now, and they're all bad.

That's impossible, Abdeslam, said Paco.

Nó, señor, it's the truth. When I see something in my head, it always happens. People won't believe me, but it's true. It happens later.

No, no. I don't believe in things like that, Paco said.

Why not? said Mercedes. How do you know what goes on inside the child's head?

I feel like going to bed, said Abdeslam.

Good night, and sleep well, Abdeslam.

He went into his room and shut the door. In his bed he lay thinking of what his life was going to be like. He had decided to have the kind of life he wanted, and he knew everything would be bad, because he had chosen the kind of life that always brings trouble with it.

The next morning he got up and let the goats out of their sheds. When he had cleaned the cows' stalls he went into the house. Paco was sitting at the table.

Paco, said Abdeslam, I'm going to stop living here. I can't stay any longer.

Why not, Abdeslam?

I don't want my father to know I'm living here with you. It's shameful to live with Nazarenes.

But you've lived here quite a while now, and you've never worried about that before.

They don't know where I am. But if they find out, they'll say: Our son, living in the same house with Spaniards, sleeping and eating there with them, and taking care of their goats and cows.

Paco knew this was not the reason, but he took out eight hundred pesetas. Abdeslam turned away, and Paco stuffed the bills into his pocket. Mercedes came in from the kitchen and began to cry. When Abdeslam saw this, he too felt like crying.

I didn't know it was going to be like this, he said. I like it here with you, but I want to be somewhere else, that's all.

When he went out Paco said to him : Remember, if you don't find any place to sleep, you can come back. Nobody else will be staying in your room.

5

Abdeslam went down to the city with the money in one pocket and a pack of cigarettes in the other. He stopped at a café in the Calle del Comercio behind the Zoco Chico, and sat at a table. The qahouaji came.

A black tea with mint, please, sidi.

While the tea was being made he lit one of his cigarettes and sat watching the people go by. A man came into the café and sat down. Abdeslam turned to look at him, and saw that he was from his own neighbourhood.

Aren't you Bachir? he asked him.

The man said: Yes. And you're one of Temsamani's sons?

That's right.

I remember you when you were only this big. What are you doing down here?

Abdeslam did not know the man, and so he could not tell him anything. You never know what's going to happen, he said. What will you have?

Bachir got up from his table and came to sit with him.

Abdeslam ordered a glass of tea for him. After the tea had come they talked for a while.

Tell me about it, brother, said Bachir. This is no place for you to be. You don't know your way around down here.

Abdeslam sighed. He was glad to have a man from his own quarter to talk to, a man who called him brother, because he needed someone who would listen while he told him everything. Bachir was nearly thirty years old. He worked as a longshoreman at the port.

Abdeslam lit another cigarette and began to talk. He told Bachir the whole story, as though his father had turned him out that very morning. Bachir sat nodding his head until he had finished.

School's not the place for you, either, he said. He should have let you stay in the mosque.

There's nothing to do now except wait for the trouble to begin, said Abdeslam.

Have you got a place to sleep?

Not yet, but I'm going to get a hotel room.

No! Bachir told him. I've got two rooms in my mahal, with a bed in each. Don't worry about anything. I'll find you some sort of work.

Wait, Abdeslam said. He liked Bachir, but it seemed too soon to settle down in another house. He had had no time yet for adventures. Let me think. There's plenty of time left before it gets dark. I'll have to think about it.

That's right. Take your time, said Bachir.

After a moment Abdeslam said : How much do you pay where you are?

A hundred pesetas a month.

I'll pay fifty. Then it will only cost you fifty.

Fine, said Bachir. He had not expected Abdeslam to offer to pay anything.

Abdeslam took out two hundred pesetas and gave them to Bachir. Here's four months' rent, he told him.

Bachir looked at the money suspiciously before he put it into his pocket. He thinks I stole it from home, Abdeslam thought.

Good. Let's go, said Bachir.

Abdeslam had not finished his tea and so they sat for a while. Then he took out his money again and paid for the two teas.

6

Abdeslam and Bachir went out of the café. They crossed
the Zoco Chico and climbed the hill into the quarter of
Benider. The mahal was at the end of a small passageway.
Bachir unlocked the door and they went into a sitting-
room with mattresses along the walls. It was quiet and dry
in the house.

They sat down and smoked.

Then Bachir jumped up. Come and look at the room,
he said. There was a mattress on a large reed mat. Above
it on the wall Bachir had hung four pictures: one of
Abd el Wahab singing, one of Bachir himself, one of some
high mountains, and one of a river with some trees along
the banks. There was a small table by the mattress, and
on the other side of the room a long chest.

Bachir brought in two blankets and threw them on to
the mattress.

And here's my room, he said. Bachir had a European
bed made of brass pipes, and there was linoleum on the
floor. In the kitchen he had a primus stove and a mijmah

for charcoal. On the wall was a photograph of a naked French girl.

They sat down again, and Bachir said : If my father had told me to get out, I'd have got out, but I wouldn't have stayed out. I'd have gone back. Even if he'd beaten me I'd have gone back. He's got to take care of you. You're too young. You can't get on by yourself.

Abdeslam looked at him. Bachir, he said, you don't understand. When he hit me I hated him so hard that I had to run away. I can't go back. Something terrible would happen. Worse than what will happen if I stay here.

Nothing's going to happen to you here, said Bachir. But in the end you'll have to go back. He's your father. You can't leave him like that. Even if you weren't his own blood, he still wouldn't throw you out for good.

I've thought about it over and over, Abdeslam told him. I don't want to talk about it. I can't go back.

We'll leave it that way, Bachir said. Now you're living here in the house. Here's your key. Each can come and go as he pleases.

Is there anything to eat? Abdeslam asked him.

Wait. Bachir got up and went out. Soon he came back with a meat and olive tajine he had bought at a restaurant. He had lettuce with him, and a loaf of bread and a litre of wine. Finally he spread everything out on the taifor and they sat down to eat. At that moment there was a knock on the door. Who is it? called Bachir.

A woman outside in the alley cried : Me !

Bachir went to the door. He came back with a woman who was wrapped in a haïk. This is Aouicha.

Hello, said Abdeslam.

She took off her haïk and her veil, and sat down on the mattress with them to eat. Abdeslam thought she was very pretty.

Bachir brought three glasses from the shelf. Abdeslam saw him coming with the bottle of wine and turned his glass upside-down. I don't drink alcohol, he told him.

You can't go on that way, said Bachir.

When they had eaten, and Bachir and Aouicha had finished the wine, they all felt good and began to sing.

After a while Bachir said : This is my day off. Aouicha, you're going to stay to dinner. I'm going out to get some food.

I think I'll go for a walk, said Abdeslam.

I'll stay here, said Aouicha. I don't feel like going anywhere.

Bachir and Abdeslam walked together as far as the Zoco Chico. Then Abdeslam went down to the Avenida de España and followed it to the end. There were not many people on the beach. The wind was cold and it whipped the sand into the air. He walked back towards the town. At last he climbed the hill to Benider and knocked at the mahal. Aouicha unbolted the door.

Did you have a nice walk? she asked him.

Yes. I was down at the beach.

All alone?

Yes.

She looked at him for a moment. Then she said : I feel sorry for you, Abdeslam. A little boy like you, all alone, and living in this place. It's not good for you. You shouldn't be here. It would be much better if you got out. Don't even sleep here one night.

And where do you expect me to go? I've paid my rent.

There are plenty of hotels where you could live without any trouble, she told him.

You see, even when I was living at home, I already knew I was going to land in a place like this, he said. I could live in a worse place if I had to. It doesn't bother me.

28

I'm afraid for you because you don't know how to be afraid for yourself, said Aouicha. You're bound to get into trouble. You'll go to jail or get killed.

Please. Let's talk about something pleasant. Who wants to talk about getting killed?

All right.

After a moment he said : It's too bad I'm not bigger. If I were eighteen or twenty I could marry you. I'd like to be married to a girl like you.

Aouicha laughed. I wish you were twenty, she said. Your face wouldn't be so pretty. That's why I'm sorry for you. There are always drunks here, and some night one of them's going after you. You haven't thought of that, have you?

Don't worry about me. I can take care of myself.

Soon Bachir opened the door. *Salaam aleikoum.*

Aleikoum salaam.

When did you get back? he asked Abdeslam.

A long time ago.

Aouicha began to get the food ready. Bachir sat down. There's a good film tonight, he told Abdeslam. We ought to see it.

Where?

At the Alcazar.

What kind?

War.

All right. Let's go, said Abdeslam.

By the time dinner was ready it was dark. They sat for a time after the meal, talking while they had tea. Then they put on their wraps and went out into the street.

At the Alcazar they sat with Aouicha between them. They bought peanuts and sunflower seeds, and the noise they made eating them was sometimes louder than the film. They did not say anything while they watched. They merely looked at the soldiers and Indians with feathers on their heads. Once in a while Aouicha would say to Bachir : Are you sleepy? Each time he would answer : No.

The film ended and they went out.

I'm hungry, said Abdeslam. I want to get something to eat. They went to the Calle de los Cristianos and ordered skewered calf's liver. Abdeslam kept saying he wanted a dozen. They carried the liver back to the mahal with them. Bachir ran ahead, and came in only a minute or so after they had arrived. He had three bottles of wine and another girl with him.

This is Zohra, he told Abdeslam.

To Zohra he said : You know Aouicha, don't you?

Zohra took off her haïk. She was younger than Aouicha, but she was fat with crinkly hair and not very pretty. The three grown-ups sat there smoking and drinking the wine that was on the taifor. Abdeslam merely watched and listened. He was looking at Bachir more than at the girls. Bachir was handsome, with curly black hair and eyebrows that met in the middle. Someone had cut his neck open at one side, so that he had a long scar beginning at his ear and going down to his shoulder. He had two coloured pictures on his right arm—a naked girl and a knife cutting a heart, with blood running out.

They sat talking, on and on, for two hours or so. Then there was no more wine. Wait, said Bachir, I'll go out and get some.

It's too late, said Aouicha. You'll never find any.

Bachir had his jacket on. I won't come back until I do, he told her.

After he had gone, Aouicha and Zohra began to talk in low voices together. Abdeslam was lying with his head back against the pillows and his eyes shut, but he was not asleep.

Zohra was saying that she did not want to stay all night with Bachir because she was afraid of him. This interested Abdeslam very much. He did not really know anything about men and women, except what he had heard the other boys say, and he could not imagine why Zohra should be afraid of Bachir. He listened carefully.

It was bad enough anyway, Zohra continued. But when he started to do that she screamed and he had to stop. And when Habiba was in the Kortobi Hospital for twelve days, that was all Bachir's fault, too. But she let him do it. It was her own fault.

I remember, said Aouicha. If you're afraid, don't stay with him. He doesn't always want that. He's used to boys, that's all.

Why doesn't he get one, then? said Zohra. I'm not going to the hospital just to give him a good time.

Aouicha did not answer. Without opening his eyes, Abdeslam knew that both women were looking at him. Poor little thing! he heard Zohra say under her breath. Then he did open his eyes a crack. He saw Aouicha shaking her head back and forth.

He shut his eyes again and went on lying quietly, and the women talked about other things. Soon Bachir returned, holding two bottles of Cachir wine above his head like two horns. He pulled out both corks, and the three of them began to drink again. Abdeslam fell asleep.

When he awoke he saw Bachir yawning and stretching.

I'm going to bed, Bachir said. He reached out and began to squeeze Zohra's breast, and she let her head fall against him. After a moment he said: Aouicha, take the boy into the other room and see what you can do with him, Zohra and I are going to bed.

Aouicha stared angrily at Bachir. Then she glanced at Zohra. Zohra had her hand on Bachir's thigh and was looking into his eyes. Aouicha jumped up and threw her haïk over her head, and went out into the street without saying anything. She slammed the door behind her.

Abdeslam stood up. He said good night to Bachir, who did not answer. He went into his room, shut the door and lay down on his mattress.

It was a shameful thing for Bachir to have said to Aouicha, even as a joke, he thought, and she was right to have been angry. Then he wondered if Zohra would have to go to the hospital tomorrow. He listened to see if she would scream. For a few minutes he heard her talking and Bachir answering, and then he fell asleep.

7

The first one up in the morning was Bachir. He went out of the house at six o'clock, so he would get to his work at the port on time. When Abdeslam heard him slam the door, he got up and peered into the other room to see if Zohra was still in bed. But the room was empty. He went to the sink and washed, feeling very much excited. Now that he had a place to sleep in the heart of the city, he was free to go and look for adventures. He made himself some coffee and ate a piece of bread that was lying there. Then he went out into the street.

It was a bright windy day at the beginning of winter. As he walked along he began to ask himself where he ought to go. I can go wherever I like, he thought, but where would I like to go? And he decided that he would make a visit to his own quarter, and go and greet Si Mohammed the baker. He walked out of the city and up the hill to the street where the oven was.

Si Mohammed was glad to see him. Come inside, he said. Where are you living now?

Down in the Medina.

Are you working?

No.

Whose house is it?

Somebody I know.

Si Mohammed shook his head. Too bad, Abdeslam, too bad.

What do you mean, too bad?

I'm afraid you're never going to amount to anything in this world.

Why not? cried Abdeslam.

Who are you living with? That's what I want to know.

Si Mohammed, I came to see you and sit where it was warm, and have a good time with you.

You're right, Abdeslam. We'll have some tea.

Si Mohammed clapped his hands. When the boy came in, he gave him money to go and get sugar and tea and mint from the bacal. Then he filled a kettle and put it into the oven. He got out the teapot and stuffed it with mint before pouring in the tea. Soon he handed Abdeslam a glass.

While he drank his tea, Si Mohammed told him what had been going on in the neighbourhood. At the end of the third glass, Abdeslam told Si Mohammed how good his tea had been, and got up. He went out, saying that he would come again one day soon.

Down in the Medina he explored the back streets for a while. He stood in the Zoco de Fuera and watched the people buying and selling. Finally he set out for the mahal in Benider.

Nobody was there. He sat down on the mattress in his room and began to listen to the silence, and after a while he found that he was crying. The part of him that had started to cry without his knowing it was saying : What am

I doing here alone? All his friends lived with their families and were happy. He told himself that he was doing what he wanted to do, but he felt afraid that he might not be big enough to do it by himself.

I've been gone a long time, he thought, to make himself feel better. And I'm going to be away a lot longer. He pictured his friends in the ruined shed, the boys he used to play with every day. But it was so long since he had been with them that he felt unsure they still existed. He knew that if he walked into the shed this afternoon and they were there, they would stop whatever they were doing and stare at him and ask him questions. He did not want to have to give any answers.

So I have no more friends either, he thought. The room grew dimmer as the afternoon came to an end. Abdeslam sat without moving.

Someone in the street was knocking at the door. He was still crying as he went and opened it. Aouicha came in. He tried to turn away, but she noticed his face.

What's the matter?

Nothing's the matter.

You've got to tell me, she said, sitting down. What are you crying about? What do you want?

I want to die, he said.

She jumped up. That's a terrible thing to say!

You don't have to tell me. I've read the Koran. It's a sin to want to die, I know. But the way I have to live now, I've got a right to want to be dead. Because whatever happens and however bad it is, I know the next thing is going to be worse.

Aouicha began to walk around the room. Abdeslam, she said, please don't cry. It hurts me to see you. Then she began to cry too. She put her arms around Abdeslam and kissed him.

35

I'll stop, he told her, and he went to the sink and washed his face. Aouicha lighted the primus. Let's have some tea and sing a little, she suggested.

I didn't know you could sing by yourself, he said. Yes. Sing something.

She began to sing a mouwal, and Abdeslam liked the low, soft sound of her voice. She sang the mouwal very slowly, inventing her own variations, so that it took a long time. When she had finished he shook his head and said : It's true. You do know how to sing a mouwal.

After Aouicha had poured the tea into the glasses she sat back. What do you know about mouwals? she asked him.

Nothing. But I like your voice. The voice is the important thing. I don't have to understand mouwals to know that.

The door opened and Bachir came in. He sat down and took a glass of tea. Then he asked Abdeslam what he had done that afternoon. Abdeslam told him he had gone to see the baker and had had tea with him.

Bachir looked sharply at him. Who is this baker? he said. Why do you go to see him?

Abdeslam was startled. He said nothing.

I wondered where you got all that money from, Bachir said. I should have known. Every pretty boy in town has money, of course.

Still Abdeslam did not answer.

Aouicha frowned. Shame, Bachir, to say such things to him!

Then Bachir laughed. I'm just talking, he said, slapping Abdeslam's knee. Don't listen to me. You know, Abdeslam, that girl sitting beside you, that beautiful little Aouicha, I want to get her into bed with me. Maybe even tonight would be a good time. What do you think?

If she gets sleepy, why not? said Abdeslam. He knew what Bachir meant, but since he did not like the idea he had to pretend not to understand.

Bachir laughed again, but Aouicha said : I'm not sleepy. You're going to be, Bachir told her.

We'll see how sleepy I get, she said. Shortly after that she got up and went home.

Bachir did not seem to want to talk to Abdeslam any more, so he went into his room and began to read once again about Haroun er Rachid.

8

That night Bachir went out. Abdeslam got his own dinner and went to bed. When the next morning he opened the door into the other room, he saw that Bachir had not been home to sleep. While he was drinking coffee Aouicha arrived and sat down with him.

Is everything all right? she wanted to know.

Of course, he said. Bachir went out right after you left and never came back.

I worry about you, you know, Abdeslam.

He laughed. Aouicha helped him clean the house and wash the dishes. When they had finished, she said: Now I'm going to make some tea and we'll sit down.

I know, said Abdeslam. We'll go to a café.

A café? she exclaimed. How can I go to a café? I'd be the only woman there. We can't do that.

But this is a special café with a big garden, and there's nobody there in the daytime.

She did not want to go, but he finally persuaded her. They walked as far as the Zoco de Fuera and took a taxi from there out to Sidi Boukhari. The café was not far from Abdeslam's neighbourhood. The sun was shining and the wind smelled of leaves burning.

Abdeslam made Aouicha wait in the taxi while he went in to speak with the owner of the café, an old man whom he knew. When he took her through the café to go out into the garden, the table was ready for them. It was behind a long screen of vines that hid it from the rest of the tables. Aouicha sat down, and Abdeslam went into the kitchen and ordered two Coca-Colas.

When the owner brought the drinks, he looked at Abdeslam and shook his head. Then he went back to the fire saying to himself : Allah ! What a shame ! That poor boy ought to be with his family. Already sitting with whores, and smoking cigarettes too. Very bad !

He worked a while, muttering to himself, and then he called out to Abdeslam. Come here, will you ? I want to speak to you.

Abdeslam got up and went in to where the man stood by the fire.

Abdeslam, my son, shame on you !

What have I done ? said Abdeslam.

I wouldn't have thought a boy like you would do such things. I saw your father in the street, and he told me the whole story.

Whatever he said, it was all lies ! cried Abdeslam. There wasn't a true word in it. I was always good, and I always did what he said. And he hit me. He drew blood ! He said : Get out and don't come back !

I know, said the café-owner, trying to talk.

Abdeslam was very much excited, and he continued : When he hit me, that was when I felt worst. When I tried to look at his face I couldn't see it. But now I've found a friend, and I have a place to live.

39

A friend? Who's that?

Bachir Zerhouni. You know him?

Yes, I know him.

That's who I'm living with now. And this is a very nice woman here with me. She's helped me a lot. Now if you'll excuse me, I'll go back and talk with her.

Of course, my son.

Abdeslam went out to where Aouicha sat behind the screen of vines. I was gone a long time, wasn't I?

That's all right, she said.

I'm sorry. The owner's an old friend of mine. He wanted to know why I don't go home. He saw my father and talked with him. What difference does it make whether he did or not? He can't make me go back!

Don't you think we ought to go soon? Aouicha asked him.

But we can get everything for lunch right here. Don't you like this café?

Of course I do, she said. It's beautiful. The garden and all the flowers. But I haven't any money and I don't want you to pay for it. And I have to be at work at two o'clock.

There's plenty of time, and I have money, said Abdeslam.

Once, years ago, I went by this place with my sister, said Aouicha. I remember looking into the garden. I thought it belonged to some Nazarene. I never knew it was a café.

Abdeslam went into the kitchen and ordered sixteen skewers of liver and lamb. While they were eating them with bread and olives, a stork flew down and began to walk around among the plants at the other end of the garden. Abdeslam watched it, laughing.

She was looking at him. Abdeslam, she said, don't you know any other boys you can go and play with?

He frowned. I don't want to play, he said.

But all boys play. Everybody plays.

No! he cried. I don't want friends to play with! I want to work and earn money.

Aouicha shook her head.

When he went to the kitchen to pay the café-owner the man said: You ought to be living with your family, not wandering around the town with women. And Bachir Zerhouni is a drunkard. A Moslem who drinks alcohol is no better than a dog. And that's what you're living with.

You're right, said Abdeslam. He did not want to talk any more. Good-bye.

The two went out into the street and Abdeslam took Aouicha's arm. She was much taller than he was. They found a taxi in front of the Spanish Consulate and took it back into the city to the nylon factory where Aouicha worked.

I'll be here at eight o'clock to collect you, he told her. You've got to have dinner with Bachir and me.

I don't want to see him, Aouicha protested.

You've got to come. Please.

Aouicha laughed and patted him on the shoulder. All right, she said.

All afternoon Abdeslam walked through the alleys of the Medina until he was familiar with many of them. He had one adventure. A man painting the front of a shop in the Calle Ibn Khaldoun splashed some paint on his sleeve. At twilight he went back to the mahal in Benider. It was dark and empty. He lighted the lamp and sat there waiting for Bachir, listening to the small children playing outside in the alley. Bachir did not come. At half past seven he set out on foot to the nylon factory. He met Aouicha outside the door and they went back to the mahal.

41

Bachir was there. Aha, Aouicha! he cried. Come in. Welcome! Abdeslam looked at him to see if he was angry with her for running out the night before, but he was not.

They sat smoking and talking for a while, and then Aouicha began to prepare dinner. While they were eating, Abdeslam said: As soon as we finish, I'm going to do a trick for you.

All right, Bachir said.

Soon Abdeslam got up and took the brazier in his hands. There's fire in there. You see? he said.

Be careful. What sort of crazy thing are you going to do with the fire?

I'm going to say three or four words, and with each word the fire will die down. And after I've said the words it will come back.

Aouicha and Bachir laughed. Abdeslam fanned the fire with the bellows and put the brazier on the taifor in front of them. He picked up two sticks and passed them back and forth over the fire as he recited a surah of the Koran.

Finally Bachir said: That game you're playing makes me nervous. Put the brazier back and play some other game, will you?

You never want me to do anything, said Abdeslam. All right, I won't do anything. I'll sit here and watch you, and you'll talk. You're old, and she's old. You're my father and she's my mother.

Bachir glanced at Aouicha.

If we go out into the street, the three of us together, people will think you're my father and mother. And if I go alone with her, they'll think she's my sister. Nobody'd ever think she could just be a friend.

Bachir laughed. You want them to think she's your girlfriend? You've got a long time to wait before anybody's going to think that.

I don't mean anything like that. I mean just a friend.

Bachir pointed his finger at Abdeslam. No woman can ever be just a friend, he said.

9

Aouicha usually worked six hours every day at the nylon factory. One afternoon a few days later she did not go to work at all. Instead, she went up to the Boulevard Pasteur and looked into the windows of the shops. In one of them she saw some animals that danced when they were wound up. She bought a fur rabbit that hopped and a fat bear that beat on a drum. Then she set out for Bachir's mahal. She knocked on the door. No one answered and so she walked on, down to the Avenida de España.

It was not long before she caught sight of Abdeslam going along under the palm trees near the park. She called his name and he turned round.

Where are you going? she wanted to know

I'm going into a bar along here to see if they have a job for me. It's a Nazarene who runs it. We'll see if I have any luck or not.

You really want to work?

Of course I want to work. My money's all gone. Only fifty pesetas. What can I do with fifty pesetas? Now I've got my rent paid, I need clothes and shoes. I need all sorts of things. And I can't get them with fifty pesetas.

Aouicha was silent a moment. Then she said : How much money do you need?

How can I tell? I know I need money, but I don't know how much.

If you need money, I can let you have it, she said.

No, Aouicha. All my life I've seen my father give money to his wives. Not them giving it to him.

That's got nothing to do with it, she said. I'll give you the money and you can buy the clothes. You don't want to get a job. I can take care of you.

He pressed her arm. Aouicha, I know you'd give me the money. But I can't take it.

As you like, she said, and pulled her haïk tighter round her head.

Here's the bar, said Abdeslam. I know a boy who works in here, and I'm going to talk to him. You wait outside.

Aouicha stood on the pavement and looked at the people while he went inside the bar. As he shut the door behind him an Englishman came up and asked him what he wanted. Abdeslam told him the name of his friend.

He's off today, said the Englishman. If you have a message for him, you can give it to me and I'll see that he gets it tomorrow.

I only wanted to see if he'd found any work for me. He promised to try and find something if he could. He told me to come by here and see him after he'd spoken to his boss.

I'm his boss, the man said, looking carefully at Abdeslam. I could use you in the bar, shining glasses and polishing furniture. The work's not hard.

Good, said Abdeslam smiling.

Tomorrow morning, then, you come at ten o'clock.

45

You'll get off at seven in the evening. That's your day.

All right. But how much do you pay?

I'll make it fifty pesetas a day.

Good.

Abdeslam went out to Aouicha.

What happened?

It's all settled, he told her. I got the job, and I have to be here at ten tomorrow. Fifty pesetas a day.

They climbed back up to the mahal laughing and feeling very happy. Abdeslam sat down and Aouicha lit the primus and put on the water to boil. Then she brought out the toys.

Abdeslam glanced at them as she unpacked them. They were for a small child. His little brother Aziz would have loved them. But he realized that he must not let her know this.

Let me see! he cried.

They squatted on the floor with the toys. Abdeslam took the bear with the drum and Aouicha took the rabbit. They wound them up and set them moving towards each other. The bear beat its drum and the rabbit jumped at it and knocked it over. It lay bumping around on the floor, still beating the drum. They laughed until it was finally still.

Abdeslam went over and picked up the rabbit to look at it closely, since he had not examined it. As he stood there Aouicha came up behind him and her hair fell against his cheek. He put his hand up and brushed it aside. At that moment she leaned over and kissed him on his lips. When she had finished she backed away and looked at him. He did not move, but stood staring at her.

When you kissed me just then it gave me gooseflesh all over, he told her.

She laughed: It's good for you.

No, I don't like the way it feels, he said. Excuse me for telling you.

Aouicha went to the sink and made two glasses of coffee. Then she came back with them and sat down on the divan beside Abdeslam.

He took a few sips of coffee. Suddenly he lay back against the cushions. I'm sleepy, he said.

Why don't you sleep a while? she asked him. I'll just sit here.

He shut his eyes. A moment later he felt Aouicha lean over and very softly take his head between her hands. Then she began to kiss him on his neck, his forehead, his cheeks, his eyes, and even at the end of his nose. He lay there with his eyes shut, his heart beating very fast. After a while, since he did not move, she got up and went to sit on a hassock across the room.

She sat without saying anything. Finally he opened his eyes.

Aouicha, he said.

What, Abdeslam?

Throw me a cigarette.

She lit him one and carried it over to him. When she gave it to him he took her hand and held on to it. Sit down, he told her.

She sat on the edge of the couch, and he pushed himself up so that he was sitting upright. Then he kissed her cheek. As his lips touched her she began to laugh. Thank you, she said.

It was getting dark in the room. Aouicha lit the lamp and came back to the couch.

I've been watching you, Abdeslam told her. And I can see you're sad about something. But I don't know what it is.

No, I'm not sad, she said. I was just thinking of when I kissed you. You weren't thinking about me. You didn't say to yourself : Aouicha's here with me, did you?

There was someone knocking at the door. Abdeslam went and unbolted it. Bachir came in with two Spaniards. This is Manolo, he said. And this is Stito. I'll be right back.

He went out. The Spaniards sat looking at Aouicha. Nobody said anything. Soon Bachir came in with two cases of beer and set them down in the middle of the floor. Then he went out again, this time to a restaurant, carrying a big basket full of empty pots and pans. He returned with the dinner, and they all drew up to the taifor and began to eat. Before they had finished eating they started to open the beer. They went on opening it, and Bachir handed a glass to Abdeslam.

No, I can't drink.

One beer's not going to hurt you.

I don't want it. I don't want any beer or wine either.

But, *hombre*! Manolo cried. We can't sit here and drink in front of you. And you not drinking?

He doesn't want to drink, and nobody's going to make him drink, declared Aouicha.

No, no! Of course not, said Manolo.

So that's settled.

They went on drinking. Bachir and the Spaniards told stories and laughed. As he sat talking with Aouicha, Abdeslam heard Stito say in a low voice to Bachir : Is this the boy?

He pretended to be busy with Aouicha, but he went on listening to the men.

He's the one I told you about, said Bachir. He's living here with me.

So I see! said Stito. You've found yourself something very special this time! *Hijo de la gran puta!*

Abdeslam looked at the Spaniard. He was thinking : Is

that Nazarene insulting me? He thought a little more. Then he said good night to Aouicha and stood up.

I've got to be at work tomorrow morning at ten o'clock, he told Bachir.

He went into his room, shut the door, undressed, and got into bed, leaving them all sitting there. It was not long before he heard the sound of bottles being smashed. He jumped up and ran to the door. Manolo and Stito were fighting in the centre of the room, and Bachir and Aouicha sat watching them. When Bachir saw Abdeslam sitting in the doorway he rose and separated his two friends. Then he firmly pushed them both out into the street.

Abdeslam shut the door and got back into bed. He heard Aouicha go out and walk quickly down the alley. Then he heard only the sound of Bachir opening a bottle of beer from time to time.

10

Abdeslam arrived at his work on time the following morning. His friend Ali was already there, and he began to show Abdeslam what his work was going to be.

During the morning he polished glasses. Later, when the customers began to come in, they sent him out to the corner to buy them cigarettes and newspapers. All afternoon he ran back and forth, and his pockets grew heavy with the coins they gave him.

When he got home that evening he sat down on his mattress to count his money. He had more than a hundred pesetas in tips. As he was sorting out the coins he heard someone knocking.

It was Aouicha. Did you go to work? she asked him.

Yes.

How was it?

Wonderful! Look at all the money I got from the Nazarenes.

I'm so glad, she said. As long as it isn't too hard for you.

No, it's easy. It's not work at all.

I've got something for you, said Aouicha. She pulled out a box from under her haïk and handed it to him.

There were some strips of metal. Then he saw that they were rails for a mechanical train, which was at the bottom of the box wrapped in tissue-paper.

How much did this cost? he asked her.

Two hundred and seventy-five pesetas.

It's fine!

Aouicha sat down on the floor and set up the rails. Then she wound up the engine and set the little train running around the track.

Do you like it?

Yes! he said. Thank you, Aouicha.

She sat watching him. He's just a child, she thought. But it doesn't matter. I still love him, even if he's too young to understand.

Can we go to a film? said Abdeslam.

All right.

They went to the Ciné Paris and saw a Spanish film. In it, a young man was in love with a girl. Both Abdeslam and Aouicha understood Spanish. This was a good thing, since the young man and the girl did not do much more than talk and sing. After the film, when they were walking in the street, Aouicha asked him: Did you like the film?

It was all right.

Yes, she said. And didn't you like the actors?

He could see that she had enjoyed everything. The girl was pretty, he said. The man was good, but I didn't like the way he sang.

When they got to the mahal Abdeslam sat down on the couch and asked for a glass of coffee. While Aouicha was making it, he ran out to a stall round the corner and bought three pastries. He made the man wrap them separately, each one tied with a silver string. Then he took them back to Aouicha and she put them on a plate.

It was funny, Abdeslam said as they had their coffee. The actor was lying back and the girl was kissing him. Like you did with me last night. You saw that film before, didn't you? And then you came and did the same thing to me.

Aouicha began to laugh. No, I never saw it before. Eat some pastry. She pushed the plate towards him.

When they had finished Abdeslam lit a cigarette and sat back smoking it.

Abdeslam, said Aouicha. Be careful of Bachir.

What?

Look, Abdeslam, she said. I want to tell you something you don't know. I lived with Bachir once. We got on all right until he tried to do something I didn't like. Something bad. I still like him, but that's all finished now.

Abdeslam did not seem to be listening. You haven't heard anything I've said, have you?

I have. You said you and Bachir used to live together.

Yes. He was like a husband. We slept in the same bed.

He was silent. It's none of my business, he said after a moment.

That's what I'm trying to tell you. I know Bachir, and I know what he likes. I'm telling you to watch out.

Abdeslam said nothing. She wants me for herself, he thought. That's why she says all this. He did not understand what she had said; to him it was the kind of nonsense women make up when they want to frighten children.

Finally he looked up at her. Come and sit here by me, he told her. Aouicha went and sat on the mattress beside him, stretching her legs out in front of her.

Your legs have hair on them, he said. And mine haven't got any.

She laughed. You're too young. When you get older you'll have hair on your legs too.

That's a funny thing. A woman with hair on her legs.

Thousands of women have hair on their legs, said Aouicha.

It's the first time in my life I've seen it.

Aouicha went on laughing. Then she leaned over and bit his ear.

And you're the first woman I ever saw biting people, too.

Be careful, she told him. Some time when people are here, don't you go telling them I bit you.

Of course not! he cried. He rose and wound up the train. Here, take it, he told her. Wait. Then he wound up the animals and put them on the floor inside the track. The train ran round and round the rabbit and the bear, until the rabbit jumped in its way and threw it off the track. There were two empty freight-cars just behind the engine, one of which he filled with crumpled scraps of paper. He went and got some pebbles out in the alley, and filled the other.

It's carrying sacks of flour and rocks, he said. Train for Larache!

Train for Ksar el Kbir! she called.

They were still playing and crawling around on the floor when Bachir opened the door. He laughed. You get on with children, don't you, Aouicha? he said. You like playing with Abdeslam.

Who else is going to play with him? she said.

Abdeslam looked at Bachir.

Don't you want her to come and see me?

Why not, if she's got nothing better to do? Did you go to work?

Yes. I made a hundred and four pesetas in tips.

That's a lot of money. I work all day at the port for eighty.

Abdeslam wound up the train. You never know what's going to happen, he said.

11

The next day Abdeslam already knew what to do when he got to the bar. He was hoping the Englishman would notice him and say something about how hard he was working, but he did not come in at all.

At the end of the day he went home. The house was empty. He sat down in the middle room to wait for Bachir. Soon he got up, lit a cigarette and began to play with the train. At eight o'clock Bachir still had not come. He decided to go out and take a walk. It was a warm damp evening without wind.

He walked and finally sat down at a small café behind the Zoco Chico where he had sat several times before, and ordered a glass of coffee. The qahouaji brought the coffee and set it in front of him, and then he said : You haven't been around lately. Have you gone back to your family?

No, said Abdeslam.

Haven't they been looking for you?

No.

The qahouaji sat down beside him and took out his

kif pipe. He filled it, smoked it, refilled it and handed it to Abdeslam.

Thanks, but I don't smoke kif, he said. Then he changed his mind and said quickly : But let me try it. I want to see what it tastes like.

He took the pipe and smoked. When he inhaled it made him cough. The smoke was sharper than tobacco-smoke. The second and third pipes he managed to smoke without coughing. He drank the hot coffee, which took the kif to his head.

Fill me another, he told the qahouaji. Before long his head was full of kif. He paid the man and went into the street. As he walked along he felt stranger and stranger, and everything looked a little different from the way he remembered it. Finally he found himself in front of the mahal.

He opened the door and went inside. The house was dark and very quiet. He heard a rooster crow from a roof near by. He lighted the lamp and sat down in the middle room. But then a terrible fear seemed to be coming towards him from all the corners of the room. He could feel it crawling through his body and making it cold. Suddenly he was angry, and he thought : Why do I have to come into this dark house at night and sit in it alone?

He looked around at the doors that led into the other rooms. He felt that there was something in the house with him, and that something awful was about to happen.

There was a knock at the door. It startled him, so that he jumped to his feet. When he opened the door he saw Aouicha. Thank God you've come ! he cried.

Aouicha looked at him and saw that he was ready to burst into tears.

What's the matter?

Shut the door, said Abdeslam.

56

They sat down on the couch.

Thank God you came! he said again. I was here alone and thinking how bad it was. Thinking how much I hate to live alone.

I know, and you shouldn't sit thinking about it, Aouicha told him.

I'll tell you the truth. I was afraid. If you hadn't come, I wouldn't have slept here. I was going out to some hotel or somewhere. But now you're here it's all right. You'll stay all night, won't you?

Have you had dinner?

No. I was waiting for Bachir, he said. You stay here and I'll bring something from the restaurant.

He took a large earthen bowl and went out to a stall that sold food. There he bought skewered lamb and fried fish. The proprietor of the stall was smoking his sebsi as he served him.

Fill a pipe for me, will you? said Abdeslam.

Are you crazy? Kif isn't for small boys, the man told him. You're too young, boy.

I've been smoking kif for years. Fill me a pipe.

The man filled his sebsi and handed it to Abdeslam. He smoked it and gave it back, without coughing. Then he took his food and went to the mahal.

A little later Aouicha said to him : What's the matter with your eyes? You look as though you've been drinking.

No! I'm not drunk, said Abdeslam. A man gave me a pipe of kif, that's all.

Why did you take it? It can drive you crazy, or give you all sorts of diseases.

Oh, I'm not going to smoke it all the time, he said. Only once in a while. Is dinner ready?

Why don't we wait for Bachir?

We can leave his for him on a plate. I'm hungry.

57

They sat down and ate. Bachir came in just as they had finished. When he too had eaten Aouicha made the tea. Then Abdeslam set up the train and started it running. What with the kif in his head, he grew very excited, and laughed until there were tears on his cheeks. Bachir! Bachir! Sit down over here! Watch!

Bachir laughed and went to sit where Abdeslam wanted him. Abdeslam wound up the bear and the rabbit and set them on the tracks so the train would hit them when it came round. He could not stop laughing. This time the train knocked both animals off the track. They lay on the floor, twitching.

Bachir was staring at Abdeslam. There's something wrong with you. You don't look yourself. You're drunk, aren't you?

No. I smoked a pipe of kif, that's all.

What? cried Bachir. So now you're smoking kif? That's perfect!

It wasn't your kif, said Abdeslam. You didn't have to pay for it.

Bachir began to shout. I'm taking care of you now, and I'm telling you you shouldn't be smoking kif.

That's what I was just telling him, said Aouicha.

Abdeslam let himself fall back on to the floor. You're both against me, he complained. You don't want me to smoke kif or anything. You're against whatever I want to do. You're not my father and mother, or my brother and sister, or anybody. You just happen to be friends of mine. And then you try to tell me what to do.

Yes, I'm a friend of yours, said Bachir. I'm trying to help you. I don't like to see a young boy like you smoking kif.

Abdeslam did not want to hear any more. He got to his feet. I'm tired. I'm going to bed. He went into his room and shut the door.

12

Abdeslam did not go to sleep right away. He shut his eyes, but instead of sleeping he listened to the voices of Bachir and Aouicha, and they made flashes of bright colours in front of his eyes. Then he thought he heard many rhaitas playing far away in some other quarter of the Medina. He did not know whether he was asleep or awake. Sometimes he thought there were fleas in the bed, and he scratched himself. Finally, he fell asleep.

In the morning he felt too tired to get up and go to work, and so he stayed in bed. At noon he made himself some coffee. A little later he went out and bought a bag of sweetmeats, and then he wandered through the alleys eating them. The air smelled sweet and everything looked clean, because it had rained. He went to the café behind the Zoco Chico and ordered a glass of coffee. The qahouaji came and sat with him the same as the day before, and Abdeslam smoked several pipes of kif. He went back to the mahal feeling very well and got into bed again.

At dusk there was a pounding on the door. It went on

for a long time. Abdeslam was in a deep sleep and he took a while to wake up.

It was Aouicha with a big paper-bag full of oranges under her arm.

I felt like having some orange juice, she said. While they were cutting and squeezing the oranges she asked him : How was work today?

I didn't go, he said.

Why not?

I didn't feel like it.

Aouicha laughed. I told you you didn't want to work, she said.

But I do. I like it. It's easy.

When they had drunk all the orange juice she said : I've got to go and sit for a while with my aunt in Metafi. I'll see you tomorrow. Here's Bachir.

Bachir came in.

I was just going, she said, and she went out.

Bachir and Abdeslam got dinner together. Afterwards Abdeslam invited Bachir to the Café Central for coffee, and they sat there all evening while Bachir talked with his friends.

The next morning Abdeslam felt wide-awake. He got up early and arrived at the bar on the Avenida de España a little before ten.

The Englishman met him at the door. I'm sorry, he said. You didn't come yesterday and I hired another boy. Here's your pay for the two days you worked.

Abdeslam walked along the Avenida de España kicking at the pavement. He was thinking : I'm sick for one day and he throws me out. That's the Nazarenes. They think people are machines.

Aouicha came to the mahal at twelve.

Now what's the matter? she cried.

Nothing. They got somebody else to take my place in the bar.

She put her arm around him. Don't feel bad about it, she said.

I feel fine, said Abdeslam. I'm just thinking of that Nazarene. That's why I look this way.

If you hadn't smoked that kif, she began.

Abdeslam shut his eyes and put his hand over his chin. Then he said : Excuse me.

What?

Just a minute. I'll be right back.

He ran out into the street and went to the café. The qahouaji was there. He sat down and ordered a glass of coffee. While he waited he smoked several pipes of kif. Suddenly he felt very light-headed.

Listen, he told the qahouaji. I'd like to work for you. It's a good café.

You would? The man sounded surprised.

Yes, I mean it.

You want to work all day?

Yes.

Come and try it tomorrow if you want. See if you like it.

That's wonderful!

He had not even finished his coffee, but he paid for it, and ran back to tell Aouicha the good news. When she asked him how much the wages were he could not tell her, because he had forgotten to ask.

13

Abdeslam's wages proved to be forty pesetas a day. Very quickly he learned how to do the work in the café. The bar had been easier and had paid more money, but at least he now had the satisfaction of being with Moslems. He watched Si Mokhtar the qahouaji carefully for a week, and then he was able to do everything in exactly the same way. Finally he was left alone in charge of the café. Each afternoon when Si Mokhtar arrived Abdeslam gave him the money he had taken in during the day. There were no mistakes.

Most of the customers smoked kif. They would come in, fill and light their pipes, and Abdeslam would go up to their tables and ask what they wanted. Then he would make the tea or coffee and carry it to them, and usually at that moment they would offer him a pipe of kif.

One pipe won't hurt me, he would answer, and he would take the pipe and smoke it. Since he was not used to smoking kif the very first pipe would go to his head, and then he would want to smoke another. Because the first pipe always calls for a second. And those two demand yet another one. Another customer would fill his pipe and offer it to him. Smoking constantly like this kept his head in a cloud all day.

Now I really enjoy kif, he said to himself, and he decided to go out and buy himself a sebsi and a mottoui. He became friendly with one man who came every day to cut his kif there in the café, and persuaded him to sell him a part of each fresh batch. This way Abdeslam always had a mottoui full of newly cut kif.

Evenings he would go home and sit with Bachir. At some point he would pull out his pipe and begin to smoke. Bachir would usually tell him that he ought to be drinking wine instead.

No, no! I don't drink, Abdeslam would say. I smoke.

Kif will give you tuberculosis, Bachir would tell him. Or a cough that will never go away. It'll make your face yellow and you won't be able to eat anything. It's a filthy habit.

I'd rather be sick and yellow than commit a sin, Abdeslam would answer. Alcohol is a sin.

One night when Aouicha was there Bachir got angry. I'm going to take that pipe and break it! he cried. And I'm going to dump the kif in your mottoui into the latrine.

Leave the boy alone, said Aouicha. She wanted to show Abdeslam that she was on his side. She thought also that kif was not so bad for him as alcohol would be. Finally it seemed to her that the less influence Bachir had over Abdeslam and the more she herself had, the better it would be for the boy.

Even with these quarrels about the kif, Abdeslam began to feel that he was settling into a comfortable life. Bachir stayed at home more often after dinner, and Aouicha came to see him almost every day. She did not kiss him and touch him any more. He was glad of this, because it had made him nervous. She kept bringing him more toys, so that now the middle room was full of them and Bachir complained.

Abdeslam worked each day at the café. He was astonished that nothing ever happened there. One day was like another. There were no adventures.

One evening while he was having his supper alone in the mahal Aouicha came in with a shopping-bag on her arm. She sat down on the divan.

Eat something with me, Abdeslam told her.

No, she said. I can't eat eggs, they're too heavy.

Then she opened the bag and pulled out a pair of flannel trousers. Try these on, Abdeslam, and see if they fit.

He was very pleased. All right, he said. When he finished eating he took the trousers into his room and tried them on. They fitted him perfectly, and he went and showed her how they looked on him. Then she held up a red flannel shirt and a black turtle-neck sweater, and finally some black shoes.

And all these are for me?

Yes, of course they're for you, she said.

Aouicha! Thank you! He was bending over, trying on the shoes, but he stood up and went over to kiss her on the cheek. Can I get you anything? he asked her.

No, I don't want anything.

I want something, though, he said.

What's that?

I feel like having some liver with garlic and red peppers and cummin, the way they make it for the Aïd el Kebir.

But you've just finished eating!

That was only eggs, he said. I'm hungry.

I can make the liver, said Aouicha. She went out to the

market and got the food. When she came back she was breathless from having hurried so fast. In less than an hour she had the food ready and on the taifor. As they were about to eat, Bachir came in with a dozen bottles of beer. Seeing the food he said : That's just what I need to go with the beer. He started to eat the liver as he drank the beer. However, there was some left for Abdeslam and Aouicha said she did not feel like eating.

When they had finished Abdeslam went into his room and got undressed. He went to the door in his pyjamas and called to Aouicha. Will you come into my room, please?

She got up and went in, and he shut the door.

I'd like to get into bed, he told her, and have you sit beside me and tell me a story.

She smiled. All right, Abdeslam, I will.

He got into his bed, thinking : Not everybody can have a girl with such a pretty face sitting beside his bed telling him stories. He lay on his back, looking at the light of the lamp on the ceiling.

I don't know whether you'll like the story, said Aouicha.

Just tell it, he said.

There was a beggar who used to go along through the streets from house to house. He would call out : Whoever gives me a piece of bread or a coin does it not for me, but only to obey the command of Allah!

One day the beggar passed by the house of the pacha, and the pacha heard his cry, and had his servants send him down a whole loaf of bread. It was such a fine loaf that the beggar decided not to eat it, and to sell it instead. He went to a Jew who paid him two bilyoun for it.

When the Jew cut into the bread he opened his eyes very wide, because there was a big diamond inside. The next day the beggar passed by the pacha's house again, and the servants gave him another loaf of bread. He took it to the Jew again. As soon as he'd bought it the Jew rushed into the back of his shop and tore it open. There was another diamond.

The Jew said to himself : Here I am, stuck in this stall making mattresses and donkey-saddles. My clothes are old, I'm dirty, and I never get a good meal. Now God has sent me someone who's going to make me rich, and it's wonderful!

The next morning the beggar passed by the pacha's house again, and got another loaf of bread. The first two days the Jew had given him two bilyoun for the bread. This morning he looked at it and handed the beggar three bilyoun.

Each day the beggar came with a loaf of bread. Soon the Jew began to give him four bilyoun. I can afford it, he thought.

At the end of a month the pacha told his servants he would like to speak to the beggar. The next morning when the man arrived and began to call out, they took him upstairs to the pacha's rooms. And the pacha said : What do you do with the bread my servants give you? Do you eat it?

No, sidi, I don't eat it. I sell it.

And where do you sell it?

To a man named Jacob who sells donkey-saddles.

The pacha sent two mokhaznia to get the Jew.

Tell me, Jacob, said the pacha, do you buy bread every morning from this beggar?

And the Jew said : Yes, your excellency. I've been buying it for a month now.

How much do you pay him for it? the pacha asked him.

I paid him two bilyoun for two days, and three bilyoun

for the next ten days, and I've been paying him four bilyoun for the past eighteen days.

I see, said the pacha. Then he frowned and said in a loud voice : Now I want you to go home and get all thirty diamonds and bring them to me!

The Jew did not dare say anything, and the two mokhaznia went back to his house with him to get the diamonds. He brought them all in the box where he had been keeping them. The pacha spread them out and counted them, and they were all there.

Then the pacha took out some coins and gave them to the Jew. Here's the money you spent for the bread, he told him. The bread is a gift.

He sent the Jew away. And then he handed the box of diamonds to the beggar. These are for you, he told him. Now you're a rich man.

The beggar didn't thank the pacha. He only said : Sidi, may you have strong eyesight, a long life, and Allah's protection from evil. Then he left.

The beggar went down the steps one by one. He was sad, because now he had no bread and no money. He held the box of diamonds in his hand. Suddenly he slipped and fell down the stairs. At the bottom he hit his head, and his blood spattered all over the wall. The servants screamed and came running, and the pacha left his rooms and went down to see what had happened. There he saw the beggar lying dead, and the diamonds scattered on the steps. Then he looked up at the wall. There on the wall, with all the letters written in the blood that had splashed out of the man's head, he saw words, and they said :

I made him poor. You made him rich.
I killed him. Now bring him to life.

Aouicha waited a little. Then she said: That's the end of the story.

Abdeslam did not answer.

Are you asleep? she asked softly.

No, I was thinking, he said.

Since he did not say any more, she asked him: Did you understand anything?

Yes.

What did you understand? she insisted.

I haven't finished understanding it! he said impatiently. You meant it for me, I know that much.

She did not notice that his voice was unhappy. You're right, she said. But the story means a lot of things.

I made him poor, said Abdeslam thoughtfully after a moment. It means you think I'm no good and can never be anything in the world. You think because I'm poor now I've got to stay that way all my life. I understand it!

Abdeslam! You're getting impossible. I didn't mean that at all. You've misunderstood on purpose. The story means all sorts of things, but it doesn't mean what you think.

I want to hear a different one each night, he said.

Not if you're going to lose your temper. If you think about it you'll see I didn't say anything against you.

Thank you for telling it. And now I'm sleepy.

Aouicha kissed him on the forehead and went back into the other room. For two nights she came and sat beside his bed to tell him a story. The evening after that they went to the cinema and he did not feel like hearing anything before he went to sleep.

14

One morning a few days later Abdeslam got up feeling
that he would like to take a long walk. If he went to work
at the café he could not do so, and therefore he decided
not to go to work and to tell Si Mokhtar that he had been
sick. It was such a fine bright day that he thought he would
go all the way up to the top of Djebel Kebir and sit in the
café at Sidi Amar.

He was out of breath when he got up there. In the
distance across the plains the mountains were covered with
snow. He sat in the garden drinking a Coca-Cola and
smoking his pipe.

By noon he was hungry and so he went back down to
the city. He had lunch at the mahal. Afterwards he went
out again into the street, hoping that he would not meet
Si Mokhtar. He walked through the gateway in the ram-
parts opposite the Jewish cemetery and climbed up to the
European part of the town. Then he wandered along the
boulevard looking into the shop-windows. Suddenly a
man stood in front of him, barring his way.

Abdeslam stopped and looked up at the man. He wore a djellaba and he did not look friendly. Where do you live? he said.

In Benider.

And your family? Where do they live?

Abdeslam hesitated, and finally he said : In Souq el Bqar.

I see. And you live in Benider. Why don't you live at home?

Abdeslam was growing nervous. Why do you ask so many questions? Who are you? he said.

It's my job to clear all you boys out of the street and lock you up. He seized Abdeslam's arm. Come on.

Let go! Take your hands off me! Abdeslam cried. But the man would not let go, and he had to let himself be led along.

The building was just inside the Casbah. When they came to the door the man pushed Abdeslam in ahead of him. Then another man asked him his name and many other things he wanted to know, and wrote all his answers down in a book. After that they took him to another room and shaved all his hair off, so that his head was white and round and shiny. They made him take a shower and then they led him into a very long room with many beds in it. A few boys were walking around between the beds. They had all had their heads shaved.

The man with Abdeslam pointed at one of the beds and told him : Here's where you'll sleep.

Yes, said Abdeslam. He sat down on the bed feeling very sad.

The next morning a boy named Abdelaziz showed him round the building and told him about the subjects they studied and the games they played. He did not listen to anything the boy told him. All he thought about was how ne could get out. In each room they went into he looked carefully at the windows to see if they could be opened, and how far it would be to jump. Abdelaziz was telling him it was a good place to live. He took him to see a room which was full of old books that were stacked on shelves from the floor to the ceiling, and to another room whose walls and floor were covered with smooth matting. This was where the boys came to pray. The dining-room had a table so long that fifty boys could sit on each side of it.

Each time Abdeslam thought how impossible it was to go out into the street, it made him feel sick. By the third day he could not eat. That afternoon when the boys were taken out to play he asked permission to go to the latrines. The Frenchman said it was all right, and he ran off down the hall. When he was certain that no one was watching him he went past the latrine door and climbed a flight of stairs to a room at the top. The door was open and the room was empty. He went in, shut the door and bolted it. Then he opened the window and climbed on to the ledge.

The roof of the next building was quite a way below, but he jumped anyway, and the whole structure trembled when he landed. He began to run along the roof. But they had seen him, and when he finally leapt from the roof down to the alley, two of the bigger boys came running out to catch him. One of them tried to grab him, but he ducked. Then the other one came after him, and he ran. He could hear the other boy coming along behind, panting.

Abdeslam went on running. He ran through the Casbah, down all the steps, and through the Medina, and did not stop until he got to the mahal. It was only when he was there in front of the door that he remembered he did not have his key. They had taken it away from him when he had arrived at the orphanage. He knocked on the door, but no one answered.

The only place to go was the port, to see if he could find Bachir. He sat down in front of the door and waited a while until he had caught his breath, and then he got up and walked down to the waterfront.

For a while he looked up and down the docks. Finally he saw Bachir, carrying a sack of cement.

So they got you to jail after all! he cried, seeing Abdeslam's shaved head.

That's right, said Abdeslam. Can you give me your key? I'll be waiting for you when you get home, and let you in.

Bachir gave him his key and he went back to the mahal. He put the water on for tea and sat down on the couch. There was no kif in his box. He left the water boiling and went out to the café.

And where have you been? said Si Mokhtar, looking at Abdeslam's head. I've been waiting for you ever since Monday.

They locked me up! For nothing! I couldn't stay there any longer, so I climbed out of the window.

Good. And are you coming to work tomorrow?

Of course. But now I need some kif, if you can spare it.

Si Mokhtar gave him four matchboxfuls. Abdeslam put the package into his pocket.

And excuse me, but I need some money too, he said.

How much?

Thirty duros.

Si Mokhtar handed him the money. You know, he said, if you're working here, they may come by and pick you up again.

There was a moqqadem sitting near by, listening. All you have to do is take the boy and get him an identity card, he

72

told Si Mokhtar. They won't make any trouble then. He can stay on and work as long as he likes.

That sounds like a good idea, said Si Mokhtar.

Abdeslam hoped Si Mokhtar would forget about it. He did not like the idea of being taken to the police for any reason at all.

15

Abdeslam went back to the mahal. The silence in the empty house made him sleepy. He lay down on his bed. He was still lying there when Aouicha knocked on the door in the evening. She had Zohra with her.

They both cried out when they saw his shaved head. We've all been so worried about you! Aouicha said.

The three sat for a while talking. Then Aouicha said: I've got something for you, Abdeslam.

She brought out a package, unwrapped it and opened the box. Inside was a four-stringed guinbri. Abdeslam took it.

Thank you! He began to pluck the strings. It was a large guinbri and it made a good deal of noise. Aouicha and Zohra laughed.

If I keep playing long enough, I'll learn how, he told them. They went on laughing.

Yes, Aouicha said. With practice maybe you could learn. A little each day. You have to sit in cafés with men who know how to play, and each one can teach you a little. In five or six years you might be able to play.

You want to see something, Zohra?

What's that?

Bring the train and the animals, he told Aouicha. She brought them all and they wound them up and set them going. When everything was running around and jumping, he began to play very loud on the guinbri. This was still going on when the door opened and Bachir came in.

What's all this? he said. It's lucky you're here, Zohra, because I'm invited to a party and I'm going to take you all with me.

Where? said Abdeslam.

On the Monte Viejo.

I can't, said Zohra, I've got to go home.

When Zohra had gone Abdeslam and Bachir went to their rooms and changed their clothes. Bachir shaved in the latrine while Abdeslam washed standing at the sink. Then, together with Aouicha, they walked up to the Zoco de Fuera where Bachir signalled to a taxi.

They drove out of the city, and up, up to the end of the road high above the sea. There the taxi had to stop, and Bachir paid the driver. When the car drove away it seemed very dark and quiet. They climbed up along a path to a small house on the hillside.

You'll sit with me, Bachir told Abdeslam, as they came near the house. Aouicha will be with the women.

At the door a man wearing a yellow turban handed Aouicha over to a woman, who took her away with her. Then the man led Bachir and Abdeslam into the courtyard in the centre of the house. There were many men sitting along the sides. At one end was a group of Aissaoua. One of them came and sat next to Abdeslam. Soon the man pulled out a kif pipe and began to smoke. Abdeslam watched him for a time and smelled the smoke. Presently he said to the man : Would you mind lending me your pipe for a minute? I left mine at home.

The Aissaoui turned and looked at him. My son, you're only a child. Much too young to smoke kif. Kif will ruin you. And he went on to tell Abdeslam all the reasons why he should not smoke kif.

I only asked to borrow your pipe, said Abdeslam. You can tell me all that after I've smoked, if you're going to let me have the pipe. I've got my own kif in my pocket.

The Aissaoui filled his pipe with his own kif, lit it, and handed it to Abdeslam. When he had smoked, he said to the Aissaoui : Your kif hasn't got enough tobacco in it.

The Aissaoui frowned at him. I gave you a pipe of kif to smoke, he said. Not for you to tell me how much tobacco it has in it.

Don't get angry, said Abdeslam. It seemed *msouss* to me, that's all, and I thought maybe you were used to smoking it that way and didn't notice the difference. So I thought I'd tell you.

Bachir was looking at the Aissaoui. When their glances met, he winked. The Aissaoui said : You're right, my boy. The kif is *msouss*. I know it. But that's the way I like it.

In summer, of course, went on Abdeslam, it's better to use less tobacco. But in cold weather you need more. He emptied the pipe and refilled it with his own kif for the Aissaoui.

The Aissaoua had begun to play their drums. Soon a woman came running into the middle of the courtyard and fell in a heap in front of the drummers. The leader went over to her and said a few words above her head. Then he returned to his place and sat down. The rhaitas began to play. After a while the woman stood up, her hair covering her face, and began to dance. And she shook up and down and swayed back and forth and kept on

76

dancing, until once again she fell face-down in front of the musicians. They stopped playing and brought braziers and threw on bakhour. The smoke was very strong.

Then the musicians started to play once again, using different rhythms, and one of the Aissaoua got up and tore off his turban. His head was shaven, but he had a long pigtail that hung down to his waist. As he began to dance, everyone who was sitting near by moved to get out of his way. Two men were trying to move the woman away from where she was lying, so that he would not trample on her, but her body rose up as if it had a steel spring inside it, and knocked them both to the ground. They jumped up, and two more helped them. Four of them managed to drag her into the house, to the rooms where the women were sitting.

Abdeslam watched the dancing. The man had pulled off his djellaba and shirt and was jumping up and down, naked to the waist. The other Aissaoua were busy bringing in armloads of cactus and thornbush, piling them in the centre of the courtyard. Soon there was a great mound. The man rushed over to the plants and began to trample them down, and then to dance on top of them. Then he lay down and rolled back and forth. In the end most of the needles were broken off in his flesh. Then he stood up and they brought him fresh cactus to chew on. When his mouth was full of blood he began to growl and bellow like a camel, and froth ran down his chin. The leader stood up with a cudgel in his hand, and he waved it at the man as if he were a camel, crying out the words a camel-driver uses when he wants to keep a camel from walking into a crowd of people. This frightened Abdeslam. He had never before seen a person become an animal in front of his eyes, and it made him feel very uncomfortable. He was not sure what was going to happen. But shortly afterwards the

77

man shut his eyes and fell over, and they carried him out. An Aissaoui began to play alone on the rhaita. The sound went on and on.

Abdeslam was no longer nervous. He relaxed and started dropping off to sleep, listening to the music of the rhaita. Afterwards a drum was beaten very softly, and he fell asleep.

Two men were carrying him. He opened his eyes and saw that they were Aissaoua, but he could not manage to say anything to them. They laid him down on the ground beside the leader.

The leader was looking at him. He was saying: Memem memem. . . .

I'm not an Aissaoui, said Abdeslam. I'm just tired. I got out of jail today. The music made me sleepy.

Everyone laughed. Abdeslam stood up. Excuse me, he said to the leader. He went back to Bachir. Let's go, he said.

You and Aouicha go, said Bachir. I'm going to stay here.

But how are we going to get back? It's a long walk and it's dark.

You can walk as far as the police station at Oued el Ihud, Bachir told him. Call for a taxi from there.

Aouicha won't like walking all the way through that forest, said Abdeslam.

Go and get her.

While Abdeslam was gone Bachir spoke with a man who was about to go back to the city, and arranged to have Aouicha and Abdeslam walk with him. The three of them went along the mountain road under the eucalyptus and cypress trees, and the wind rattled and whistled over their heads. The man had a torch. Aouicha walked on one side of him and Abdeslam on the other.

16

Later, when Abdeslam and Aouicha were at the mahal, he began to talk excitedly. See where he took us, he cried. To look at somebody eat thorns, to watch a lot of crazy people! What kind of a party was that?

Why, what's wrong with that? she said.

Why should anybody hurt himself? How can a man want to cut his own body? Who wants a thousand thorns in his back?

Nobody wants it, she said. But they do it. They can't help it. Nothing can stop them.

But that's terrible, said Abdeslam.

You're just a boy. You don't know anything yet.

These words hurt Abdeslam. I know plenty of things, he told her. I know more than you do. And I'm not a boy, I'm a man. I feel as if I were thirty or forty years old.

You may feel that way, she said, but nobody else thinks anything of the kind. I just see a pretty little boy sitting there.

Maybe, but inside my brain I'm not like that. Whatever

words anybody throws at me I can throw back, and more besides.

Of course, Aouicha said impatiently. But I'm not talking about that. I'm only talking about the Aissaoua. You see what I mean when I say you don't understand anything. I'm talking about the Aissaoua and you're talking about people insulting each other. We're not having an argument. We're talking about the Aissaoua.

I'm talking about the Aissaoua too. But you began talking about me. The Aissaoua are nothing to me. Just savages.

Yes, said Aouicha, yawning.

Of course you might be right and I might be wrong, he went on, hoping to prolong the discussion. Because I've never been right from the day I was born.

What do you mean, you've never been right?

When I was little I was never right because I was little. And now I'm big and I'm still not right. It's always other people who are right. If I were right, I wouldn't be living here in this house with the kind of people who come here. I'm too old to play games in the street, and I'm too young for everything else. And I'm not doing anything I want to, and time goes by, and I'll never get anywhere.

Why are you saying all this? What's the matter with you?

That's what I want to know. That's the big thing I can't find out, what's the matter with me. If you know, tell me.

If you'd listened to your father you wouldn't be here, said Aouicha. That's the answer. That's all that's the matter with you.

Yes, he said.

Then he corrected himself and cried: No! Everybody tells me that. It's not true. If I'd listened to my father it would all have happened just the same. If your life's going to go wrong, it'll go wrong no matter what else happens. You can't escape. You're still alive and you have to go on living, whether you're happy or unhappy.

Aouicha sighed. It's true, she said. Wouldn't you like something hot to drink? Or something to eat?

No! he cried. I don't want anything. And I'm going to bed. My feet hurt.

Aouicha jumped up. What's the matter with you? she said angrily. I ask you if you want something and you walk out. What is it that's put you in such a bad mood?

Please, Aouicha, don't yell at me. That's why I'm not at home with my family, so as not to have to listen to people yelling at me any more.

I'm sorry, she said.

That's all right. Only don't start again. I forgive you.

Abdeslam walked to the door of his room. Then he turned and said: I always forgive everybody, whether they deserve it or not. Good night. Thank you for shouting at me.

I said I was sorry, she told him.

Thank you for saying you're sorry.

He shut the door and got into bed.

17

Aouicha went on sitting alone in the middle room, wondering why she had been angry with Abdeslam and wishing she had not shouted at him. Poor child, she thought, now he's hurt and he's lying in there feeling unhappy. I should never yell at him. I'm a grown woman and he's a little boy. Why can't I remember that? She felt that it was absurd for her to be so quickly upset by a child, and she was ashamed of herself.

I'm twenty-eight and he's only twelve or thirteen. I wonder if I ought to go in and comfort him, she was thinking.

She got up and opened his door. The lamp was still alight. Abdeslam was lying on his back with his eyes open. She leaned over him. He did not look at her.

Abdeslam, what's the matter with you? Tell me.

Nothing's the matter.

You're angry because I yelled at you?

No, he said.

I know it's that! she cried.

No. When you yelled I felt wonderful. I love to be yelled at.

I'm sorry.

I told you I forgave you, he said.

Do you want me to go home?

You can go or you can wait for Bachir.

Bachir won't be back tonight, said Aouicha. He'll stay at the party.

Abdeslam yawned. It doesn't matter to me, I'm going to sleep. And you can go or stay, whatever you want. You're not tied to a stake like a goat.

It's the kif! Aouicha cried. That's what makes you like this! You weren't this way before you began to smoke so much kif.

And you're drunk, he said. You drank wine before you went to the party.

Aouicha bent down and turned the lamp very low. She began to wander around the room in the dim light. Abdeslam was sleepy and was not watching her. Suddenly he saw that she was taking off her clothes. He could not say anything. He lay silent and watched her undress.

She stood there naked for a moment, looking at him. It was too dark to see the expression on her face. Then she climbed into the bed with him, and ran her hand very lightly along his thigh.

Aouicha, don't do that, please.

Why not?

It gives me gooseflesh. I don't like it.

Gooseflesh?

Yes. I told you before.

And if I should put both hands on you, what would happen?

I don't know, he said.

She slipped her other hand under his pyjama-top and

ran it over his chest, and she went on rubbing his thigh softly. How do you feel now? she asked him.

I've got still more gooseflesh, and I feel as though my head had come off.

She laughed. What do you mean? Your head has come off?

It's the way you move your hand on my skin, he said. It makes me feel like that. I don't like it. It makes me shiver.

That's the way I want you to feel, she told him.

You do? he said.

Yes. She kissed him and put his hand on her breast.

In the midst of this strange dream, when Abdeslam was no longer sure of what was happening, he suddenly saw that Aouicha had changed. She seemed to be falling into a trance. She clung more and more tightly to him, and soon she was moaning. He did not know what was wrong with her. It frightened him and made him think of the man who had changed into a camel. She's having an attack, he thought. It's her own fault.

Finally she became calm, and he said : I'm sleepy.

Go to sleep, she said, and kissed him.

He turned over and faced the wall, thinking : She's made me commit a sin. A terrible sin.

Aouicha blew out the light.

18

In the morning Aouicha got up early, made breakfast for
Abdeslam and went home, leaving the food ready for him
in the middle room. Soon afterwards Abdeslam got up. He
ate the food without stopping to think that it had been
Aouicha who had prepared it. Then he began to think
about her, and about the sin of the night before. He
decided that he could not go to work, and that the best
thing now would be to read the Koran for a while.

He brought the book from a small table in the corner.
It was a second-hand copy that he had bought one day
in the Joteya. He opened it and began to read aloud from
it. Beside him on the taifor lay his kif pipe and his kif,
and an ashtray, with water in it. At the start, before the
kif got into his head, he read in a low voice. But before
long he was chanting at the top of his voice. Reading the
Koran is like going into a trance or dancing until you
drink your own blood. It begins slowly and gets hotter
and stronger until the person doing it does not know who
he is.

Abdeslam went on for a long time, chanting very loud. There were two windows in the middle room, and they were open. One of the neighbours who lived behind the mahal was sitting with his family, listening. The people called him El Fqih, because he was a great Koran reader, and often invited tolba to come and read in his house. After listening for some time, El Fqih said to his wife: Very strange, coming from that house. A good voice, too. It's a young boy. And the boy seems to understand what he's reading.

Soon El Fqih sent one of his sons to Bachir's house. He pounded on the door. Abdeslam went and opened it.

Good morning, said the boy. Who's here in this house?

Nobody. I'm alone.

Who was reading the Koran?

I was. Why?

Nothing. My father was listening, and then he asked me to go and see if I could find out who it was. That's all. Excuse me for bothering you.

The boy walked down the alley. Abdeslam shut the door. He put the Koran away and began to chant from memory. And he finished the surah.

The boy went back to his father. Who was it? El Fqih asked.

Just a boy like me.

Living in that house? Very strange, said El Fqih. Tomorrow the tolba are coming, incha' Allah, and we've got to invite that poor boy.

Yes, Father.

Abdeslam felt like going out into the street, but he sat thinking. He had no money and he was ashamed to go to the café now, because he had not gone at the usual hour. Finally he decided to go anyway.

When he went into the café Si Mokhtar looked at him

in surprise. Did something happen? he asked him. Why are you so late?

I felt sick when I got up, and after a while I felt better, so I came.

Si Mokhtar looked at him and said: Yes. Your face is a little pale. I'm glad you feel better. Today's Friday, isn't it?

Yes.

I want to go to the cemetery at Bou Araqía to see my father and mother, said Si Mokhtar. To sprinkle some water on the graves, and have a taleb read a little for them.

Let me go with you, Abdeslam said. You don't need a taleb. I'll read for them.

Si Mokhtar knew that Abdeslam read the Koran better than many tolba. A very good idea, he said.

Under the archway at the entrance to the cemetery people sat selling bunches of raihane. Si Mokhtar bought some, and they carried the plants inside and put them on the graves. There were a great many people coming and going, the same as in any cemetery on Friday. Abdeslam settled himself on the ground and began to chant in a loud, ringing voice. The people who had come there to visit their relatives all turned their faces to look at him. Three tolba who had been talking some distance away came towards the grave and sat down to listen. Then they started to chant together with Abdeslam. When he paused to catch his breath they would continue the chanting. After he had finished he got up and went to greet and bless the tolba.

Abdeslam, my son, said Si Mokhtar as they walked out of the cemetery, how can any boy know so much of the Koran and not go on studying?

Abdeslam did not reply.

They went back down into the Medina and sat in the

87

café smoking great quantities of kif. In the back of Abdeslam's mind was the picture he had of himself and Aouicha, and of the forbidden thing they had done together. He did not need to ask anyone in order to be sure it was a sin, but he was not certain now how much of the blame was his and how much was Aouicha's.

Si Mokhtar was telling him about his own life, and how the same things had happened to him as had happened to Abdeslam. He had left home, slept in the street, travelled to many foreign lands, been put in jail, and finally had worked and earned money. And he had bought two houses as well as the café.

I don't earn anything here, you know, he said. I like to sit here and see the people. That's why I keep the café. I can't sit at home doing nothing all day.

You've had a hard life, said Abdeslam.

Yes, son, I have.

Although I don't think it's been as bad as mine is.

I don't know about that, said Si Mokhtar. I wonder.

Tell me the truth. My life's worse, isn't it?

Yours is worse, I suppose, because you're a child, said Si Mokhtar. I lived at home until I was seventeen. That's the big difference. I was already a man when I ran away. And then I had a fight, and I went to Algeria. I got married there. That's the wife I have now. By the time I came back here I was forty. I had some money, and I bought the houses. Everything's all right now, hamdoul'lah.

Yes, said Abdeslam. You ran away at seventeen and married and bought houses. They never let me get to be seventeen. If I'd got to be seventeen I could have beaten somebody up, too, and run away and got married and made money. But it doesn't matter. I'm alive and well, and I don't need anything from anybody.

I wonder, said Si Mokhtar. For a while he did not speak.

88

Then he said : How would you like it if some day I should adopt you? You could live with me and my wife just as if you were our own son. What do you think? Do you think you'd like that?

I don't know, said Abdeslam.

And then later on I'd leave you one of the houses and the café. I'd put them in your name. Or if I lived long enough, and you were ready to get married, I'd look for a girl for you. A bright girl of a good family, who knew how to read. You'd have a happy life, with a fine wife and children.

But I'm not thinking of being married or owning houses and cafés, objected Abdselam. I wouldn't want to live like that. When I grow up, if I live, incha' Allah, I want to build my own café and my own house. Or even my own hotel. I want to do it by myself, with my own ideas and my own hands. You know, Si Mokhtar, whatever you don't pay for yourself always does you harm. Only sin comes free of charge.

Si Mokhtar was looking at him with astonishment. He did not say anything.

Excuse me for not thanking you before I explained, said Abdeslam.

You didn't say anything wrong.

I always say something wrong, but I don't mean to.

No, no, said Si Mokhtar. I understand. I was just talking anyway.

Soon a boy came into the café with a basket. Here's your lunch. Your wife sent it, he said.

Si Mokhtar took out a casserole full of lamb cooked with olives, and a loaf of white bread, and they sat down to eat. When they had finished they began again on the kif, and drank more glasses of coffee. Then Abdeslam decided to speak. I need a little money, he said.

89

What do you need money for?

You don't have to ask me that. All you have to say is : I'll lend it to you, or : I won't.

I can't say I haven't got it, said Si Mokhtar. But I can ask why you need it. Anyway, it doesn't matter. He got up and without saying any more took out three hundred pesetas and gave them to Abdeslam.

Thank you very much. He put the money into his pocket. I've got to go now, he said.

I hope you'll be all right tomorrow, said Si Mokhtar. Remember, I think of you the same as if you were one of my own family. If you'd only live with the right kind of people you could stay the way you are now, a good boy from a good family.

But I don't want to stay the way I am now! cried Abdeslam.

You say you won't come and live with me and my wife, said Si Mokhtar. But at least let me go to your father and talk to him. I can arrange it. And then you can go home where you belong. That's the only place where you'll be happy. You can't go on like this, Abdeslam. It hurts me when I think of you living the way you are.

I'm not doing anything, Abdeslam protested. He thought again of last night's sin with Aouicha.

I know how you're living, said Si Mokhtar.

If you want us to go on being friends and respecting each other, you'll have to do me a favour, Si Mokhtar.

What's that, Abdeslam?

Don't go and see my father, and don't tell me ever again to go back home. I won't go back. Not as long as I'm alive. And I'm still alive! It's half past three. I'll see you later, or tomorrow. Good-bye.

19

Abdeslam felt as if he were floating when he went out of the café. The kif was singing in his head. He passed by the Djemaa el Jdida and followed the streets down as far as the Saqqaya. The women and children made a noise filling their pails at the fountain in the square, but above the sound he heard men playing music in a café. He stopped and listened and decided that he liked the piece. He had never been in that café before, but he climbed the stairs and took a seat. There were men sitting here and there, and up on the soudda, higher than the customers' heads, sat a group of musicians wearing djellabas and turbans and old-fashioned Djebala trousers. One of them had a large guinbri, one had a tenibar, another a violin, and there were others with drums and tambourines. And a young person wearing a kaftan with a gauze dfin over it was dancing and singing. Abdeslam could not tell whether it was a girl or a boy. As he entered, the musicians spoke to each other about him in special lines that they added to their song. Here's a new boy. He was never here before, they were singing. He understood this, but then they sang more about him, using words that he did not understand.

The qahouaji came up to him and said : Good evening. What will you have?

A Coca-Cola. Very cold.

The qahouaji brought it. At the same time the dancer came up to his table and bowed low before him. Abdeslam merely stared. A man sitting near by called to him. Don't you know what he wants?

No, said Abdeslam. Is it a boy?

He's asking you for something.

Abdeslam put his hand into his pocket, took out five pesetas, and gave them to the dancer, who moved quickly into the centre of the floor and went on dancing.

A man handed Abdeslam a pipe of kif. He smoked it, filled the bowl from his own box, and gave it back. Everyone was happy. There was music, singing, dancing and kif to keep everything right. Finally Abdeslam said good night to the men around him, paid for the Coca-Cola and went out. By this time he felt as light as the air itself. Soon he was back at the mahal. He did not know whether he wanted to hear Aouicha's knock at the door or not. He lay down on the floor and played with his toys, but he had so much kif in his head that he kept jumping up and going into the other rooms, as if he thought he might find someone in there to talk to. Then he sang for a while, and in the midst of his singing Bachir walked in and stood looking at him, swaying back and forth. He had been drinking brandy.

Ah, you're here, Bachir.

I'm here.

You're early.

Yes. I've got a friend with me.

He pulled a young man into the room. This is Hamidou.

Abdeslam said: How are you? But the other only grinned and sat down on the divan.

I see he smokes kif, said Hamidou to Bachir, as if Abdeslam were not in the room at all.

Does it bother you? Abdeslam asked him.

I see he has a lot to say, too, Hamidou went on.

Yes, I talk and smoke kif. And a lot of other things besides, said Abdeslam. But I don't drink brandy.

Hamidou still paid no attention to him. You've got to do something about this one, he told Bachir. You've got to take him in hand.

Bachir laughed. You're right, Hamidou. He needs a night with me. That would set him on his feet.

Hamidou reached out his hand and clasped Bachir's hand in agreement. It takes a man to teach a boy what he needs to know, said Hamidou. You can't leave it to a woman. She'll only teach him what she wants him to know.

Bachir shouted with approval, and they shook hands again, laughing.

Abdeslam did not entirely understand what they were saying, but he knew they were talking about him.

I don't need anybody to tell me what I have to know, he said.

Hamidou laughed louder. Bachir looked at Abdeslam fixedly for a moment, and then said: That wouldn't surprise me.

Abdeslam had had enough of being laughed at, and so he got up and took his pipe and kif into his room and shut the door. Not long afterwards he heard the front door shut. He supposed that the two men had gone out, and so he went back into the middle room and sat on the divan to smoke. Then he looked up and saw Bachir coming out of the latrine, fastening his trousers.

93

I thought you'd gone out, he said to Bachir.

Bachir did not answer. He walked crookedly to the other side of the room and sat down on a hassock. Then he stared at Abdeslam, and went on staring.

Suddenly he said: Abdeslam.

Yes?

When are you going to spend the night with me?

Abdeslam looked at him. Bachir, please, he said. If you want us to go on being friends, don't say things like that to me.

Bachir sneered. Is the poor little thing upset already?

Abdeslam's face turned red. I'm not a woman, he said. Why do you make jokes like that?

Bachir sneered again.

I respect you. And I trust you. You're a man, and you know my father. But I don't like that kind of joke.

I didn't say anything, did I? said Bachir. What's so terrible about sleeping with me one night? Does it scare you so much?

Stop it, Bachir!

Bachir stood up. So did Abdeslam.

One of these nights you're going to lie in my bed with me all night long. So you'd better get used to the idea. If I have to force you, you're not going to like it at all. You come of your own accord. Then you'll like it.

Never! cried Abdeslam. You'll never be able to make me do it.

Bachir reached out and gave Abdeslam a push in the chest with his hand, so that he fell backwards. Don't say never to me! he shouted.

Someone knocked. Bachir opened the door. It was one of the men who worked at the port with him.

Ahilan, Bachir! He came in and sat down. Who's this? he said, pointing at Abdeslam.

94

A friend of mine, Bachir said, holding out a packet of cigarettes to the man.

Ah, you mean a close friend?

More or less like that.

No! cried Abdeslam. It's not true! It's not like that!

Maybe not yet, Bachir said. But it's going to be like that, I tell you! Sooner or later you're going to be in that bed in there with me. And when you're there, remember what I told you.

He turned to his friend. Let's go.

Bachir pushed the man into the street, followed him out and slammed the door.

It was quiet in the house once more.

Abdeslam sat down on the divan and looked at the floor. Aouicha had turned out to want something when she had first kissed him. Now he understood that Bachir was not joking at all, and that he too wanted something. He shut his eyes and remembered Aouicha's words to Zohra: Bachir's used to boys. It had not meant anything then. Now he thought: He uses boys as women, that's it.

There was a bad time ahead. After a while he found himself crying quietly.

When the tears had cleaned the kif from his head, he was able to think again. He told himself that he must learn to live without crying. If he could get used to being unhappy, he thought, he would not cry any more. Then he went into his room, knelt on the floor and prayed to Allah to let him live until he was fifteen. By then he would be strong enough to fight Bachir.

I can't do anything to him now. I've got to wait. Some day when I'm big I'll walk up to him and tell him: Now say it. Say you want me to spend the night with you.

He sat for a while on the floor thinking of the things he would do to Bachir. Finally he got up and made some

95

coffee. With the coffee he smoked several pipes of kif. Suddenly he sprang up and set the train and the animals running. He sat on the divan playing the guinbri while the things moved, feeling top-heavy with the kif. When he had played enough he sat up and began to chant the Koran.

He had been chanting for more than an hour when someone rapped on the door.

Bismillah, he said under his breath. Maybe this one will bring luck, whoever it is.

He opened the door. It was the son of El Fqih the neighbour, with a basket on his arm.

My father sent this to you, the boy told him. Tomorrow, incha' Allah, he wants you to come to our house. At three in the afternoon.

All right, said Abdeslam. He took the basket from the boy and shut the door.

There was a tajine of lamb, eggs, almonds and onions, and with it there were two loaves of bread. While Abdeslam was eating he remembered how, when he had been studying at the mosque, if a man brought food the fqih always blessed him, and the boys cried: Amin! in chorus. And he went and sat near the window and chanted a surah. He was sure the man could hear him. When he finished the surah he chanted his blessing. Then he sat back and thought of other sections of the Koran, the ones that dealt with the sin of drinking alcohol.

It was nine o'clock. He felt that Aouicha might knock on the door and he jumped up, afraid that she would come before he could get out of the house.

He went to the café. What are you doing here so late? said Si Mokhtar.

I didn't feel like sleeping. Abdeslam sat down in one chair and put his feet up on another. Si Mokhtar sat opposite him. They drank coffee and smoked kif until after midnight. At one point Abdeslam's eyes closed and he fell asleep. Then Si Mokhtar went and sat in the dark corner by the fire. There were only three men left in the café, and they were not talking together. It was very quiet.

What a shame! Si Mokhtar said to himself, thinking of the way in which Abdeslam was living. If he were only my son I could save him. I'd educate him and make a happy man out of him.

Then he shrugged, remembering what Abdeslam was really like, and how he always refused to listen to what anyone had to say to him.

He couldn't sleep at home, and so he came here to sleep, he was thinking. But why? Why couldn't he sleep at home?

Abdeslam went on sleeping in the same position, sitting in one chair with his feet up on the seat of the other. Si Mokhtar did not want to disturb him. The customers left, and Si Mokhtar shut the café. Then he went and lay down on his mat, pulled a blanket around him and slept. He did not usually pass the night in the café, but for this one night he did not mind doing so, because he felt that he should let Abdeslam go on sleeping.

At half past five in the morning Si Mokhtar got up and began to build the fire and clean the café. Abdeslam slept until half past eight. He had a pain in his back when he woke up, but it went away when Si Mokhtar gave him some breakfast. He decided to tel Si Mokhtar that he still felt sick.

You'd better go home, Si Mokhtar told him. Maybe you'll feel better later.

Abdeslam walked back to the mahal.

He unlocked the door and went in. There was a woman without any clothes lying asleep in Bachir's bed. When she heard him she awoke and pulled the covers up over her.

What are you doing here? she cried. Who are you?

You mean, who are *you*? said Abdeslam.

I'm a friend of Bachir's. How did you get in?

I'm a friend of his, too, he said, and he waved the key in his hand.

What do you mean, a friend of his? the woman said. You mean you sleep with him?

No, I don't sleep with him, he told her. He's a friend of mine. He knows my father. I pay half the rent here.

The woman began to laugh. Are you Abdeslam?

Yes.

When Bachir got up this morning he was yelling all over the house for you. But I didn't know you were just a baby.

I slept in a café, said Abdeslam.

He went into his room. In a few minutes the woman had dressed and was sitting on the divan in the middle room. Abdeslam went and sat on a hassock opposite her, and looked at her.

You know, he said, with that zigdoun and those big trousers and your short hair, you look just like a gorilla.

What do you mean? she cried. I've never seen such a rude boy!

It's true you're not pretty, he went on. I know it's not your fault. But you're disgusting, and that is your fault.

The woman drew in her breath noisily. Abdeslam said: But that's what Bachir likes. He's never yet brought a pretty girl in here. They're all like you.

The woman stood up.

You filthy little zamel, she said. I hope Bachir rips you in two! She turned and went out.

20

Before Abdeslam went to El Fqih's house that afternoon he washed the dishes and pots that El Fqih had sent with the food. Then he put them into the basket the boy had brought them in.

The tolba were already there sitting on the floor when he arrived carrying the basket. He kissed El Fqih's hand and went to sit with them. They chanted one by one. Abdeslam's turn came, and he chanted a surah about sin. When he had finished, the chief taleb said to him: May you die open-eyed and without fear! I've never heard a small boy chant like that.

After they had all finished chanting, together they said: Allah akbar! three times, and tnen: Salaam aleikoum! three times. El Fqih sent for henna, and they rubbed it on Abdeslam's right hand. A few minutes later they brought water and soap and washed it off, but the colour remained on his skin.

El Fqih sat down by Abdeslam and began to talk to him. That house you're living in is no place for you, he told him. I've seen the women who go in there. They're vicious women. They can do you great harm.

Abdeslam saw that El Fqih wanted to interfere with his life. He frowned and said : I get very nervous when I hear people talking about other people behind their backs.

You're right, my son, and may Allah forgive me, said El Fqih. I'm sorry I mentioned the women. You seem like a bright boy. Haven't you got a father?

I have a whole family, said Abdeslam.

Then what are you doing in that house? Tell me that, at least.

I'm there because in that house I don't have to study French! Abdeslam cried.

El Fqih did not seem to understand, and Abdeslam decided that this was the moment for him to leave. He excused himself and went back to the mahal.

In his room he sat down on the bed with his pipe and kif on the taifor in front of him and began to smoke seriously, one pipe after another. As he smoked, he was thinking that he had had enough of living with Bachir. He's spent his whole life in the port, carrying sacks of cement, he said to himself. He can't read, or even talk, because he doesn't know anything. What right has he got to tell me I've got to sleep with him in his bed? I haven't done anything to him.

While he was sitting there he heard the door open. Bachir had come in.

So you're here? said Bachir.

Abdeslam stood up. Yes, I'm here. Please, can I speak to you a minute? Just a few words.

What about?

I pay my rent here and I help you with a lot of things in the house. I don't understand why you talk to me the way you do.

What's this about? What have I said?

You know what you said last night. About making me sleep in your bed even if you had to beat me up.

I see. And you don't like the idea of being beaten up? No.

Then you'd better come of your own free will.

Never!

Bachir drew back his arm and slapped Abdeslam's face so hard that he fell. On the way he hit an iron stool and it made a gash in his arm. He lay on the floor, looking up at Bachir, trying not to cry.

You saw I was smaller than you, he said, so you felt strong and hit me. Now you feel even stronger.

Shut up! Bachir told him, shaking his foot in Abdeslam's face. I'll grind you into paste.

Abdeslam picked himself up off the floor. There was an earthenware dish on the table beside him. He seized it and threw it at Bachir, but he missed. Then he ran to his room, with Bachir after him. At that moment there was a knock on the door. Instead of following Abdeslam into his room, Bachir went to open the door. Allal, a friend of Bachir's, came in. He had to step over the pieces of the broken plate. Bachir was panting, and Abdeslam was crying in his room.

What's the matter with the boy? What's going on?

The little son of a whore! Bachir shouted. After all the favours I've done him! After all the food he's eaten and the clothes he's had!

Abdeslam came running back into the room. It's a lie! he screamed. You're the son of a whore, not me! You hit me and knock me down because you're a man and I can't stop you. I pay my rent and I buy my food. You never buy anything. And what clothes did you ever give me? You didn't pay for any of them!

Bachir began to laugh. I know, but Aouicha did.

And she's my friend, not yours!

Bachir laughed louder. Maybe some day she will be, he said. Not yet.

And some day I swear by Allah I'll meet you when I'm big enough to kill you.

No, no! cried Allal. Bachir's your friend. You shouldn't talk like that. Don't swear by Allah and don't talk about killing people.

It's his fault, said Abdeslam. He's always telling me I've got to sleep with him, and I don't want to. That's why he hates me, because I won't do it. And I never will. He'll have to kill me first.

Bachir's just having a joke with you, Allal told him. Can't you see that?

Look at all the women there are in the street, went on Abdeslam. He can bring home any woman he wants. He can bring home boys if he likes, all the zouamel in the city. I don't care who he has in his bed with him. Why does he have to come after me?

Don't worry about it, Allal said. He doesn't mean it.

Bachir and Allal made a tajine of swordfish and red peppers, and Abdeslam sat quietly, watching and smoking his kif. The two men drank a good many glasses of wine while they worked. From time to time Abdeslam would get up with the bellows and fan the coals in the brazier for them. And sometimes he would hand Allal a pipe of kif and Allal would smoke it, nodding his head in thanks and refill it with his own kif and pass it back to Abdeslam. When the tajine was cooked they took it off the brazier and set it on the floor. After a while it had cooled off, and they began to eat.

When the meal was over Bachir went out into the street to buy more wine. Once that had been finished off, he was very drunk. He began to look again at Abdeslam. Presently he said to Allal : Isn't he a beauty?

Leave the boy alone, Allal told him. Can't you see that's no way to do anything? You'll never get anywhere like that.

Bachir was not listening. He stood up, still looking at Abdeslam. A beautiful boy. It's the truth.

He was swaying a little from side to side. Abdeslam leapt up with an empty wine bottle in his hand. As he waved it above his head he suddenly kicked Bachir in the stomach. It was not a hard kick, but it sent Bachir off-balance, so that he fell back on to the divan.

Abdeslam ran to his room, the bottle still in his hand, slammed the door and bolted it. Then he stood listening with his ear against the door.

I'll fix you tomorrow! Bachir was shouting. I'll shit on your mother!

You won't do anything, you son of a whore! Abdeslam cried.

I'll just kill you, that's all.

And if you do, the next time you get drunk I'll cut your head off!

In the morning, after listening at the door a good while, Abdeslam opened it and peered out into the middle room. The house was empty. Bachir had gone to work. He dressed quickly and hurried out to the café.

When he had drunk his coffee and eaten his croissants he sat back and said to Si Mokhtar : I'm ready to work.

Very good, said Si Mokhtar. That gives me the chance to go home right now. He put his things into a kouffa and went out, leaving Abdeslam in charge of the café.

In a very few minutes he was back. Abdeslam, he said, I forgot to tell you. We're going to do something.

What's that?

From now on you'll stay here alone all day serving the customers. And in the afternoon when I come, whatever money is in the cash-box we divide between us. If there's a hundred pesetas, it's fifty for you and fifty for me. And if there are two hundred, it's a hundred each. How's that?

It's a wonderful idea, said Abdeslam. Thank you.

That's all I came back for, to tell you that, said Si Mokhtar. He went out into the street again.

21

When Bachir had finished his work at the port he went to a bar on the waterfront and had some drinks. He was still angry with Abdeslam when he went back to the mahal. The house was empty, so he went directly to the café. He walked in and went up to Abdeslam.

Now I'm going to fix your mother for you, you little shit!

It's your mother you're talking about, Abdeslam said I'm busy working here. You'd better not make any trouble.

There were two young drunks sitting there. They got up and went over to Bachir. What do you want with the boy? they asked him, and they began to push him around and were about to hit him, but Abdeslam asked them not to.

Thank you for your help, he told them. You see how big he is and how small I am. When he's sober he can hit me, but when he's drunk I can hit him.

Bachir grunted and went out.

In the afternoon Si Mokhtar came, and they went over

the accounts. Abdeslam had taken in two hundred and eighty-four pesetas during the day. After expenses had been taken out he had a hundred and seventeen for himself. He was happy when he put the money into his pocket. He went to a bacal and bought bread, sugar, butter, tea, mint and milk.

When he got to the mahal he found Bachir sitting with an old Spanish woman and three young men. Bachir paid no attention to him, but he went round and shook hands with them all, the three young men first and then the old woman. When he got to her she would not let go of his hand.

Sit down here by me, gazelle, she said.

Abdeslam pulled his hand away. Does it matter whether I'm a gazelle or a donkey? he said. Do you care?

Why are you so sulky, gazelle? The old woman fished in her handbag. Here. Here's five pesetas. Go and buy some candy.

Abdeslam stared at her in surprise. I'm not thinking about your pesetas, señora, he said.

Oh. And what are you thinking about?

Just one thing. Bachir.

This Bachir here?

He keeps saying he's going to beat me up. I haven't done anything to him. And he hits me and then laughs at me because he's stronger than I am.

The Spanish woman turned to Bachir. You don't really treat him like that, Bachir. You didn't really hit him, did you? She reached out her arm and stroked the back of Bachir's neck.

Yes, I hit him, said Bachir. I know. I won't do it again.

I hope not. You can't treat children that way.

It's all right, Abdeslam told the woman. I forgive Bachir for four or five years.

Bachir laughed and Abdeslam turned to face him. Perhaps by then I'll be a drunk too, and we can sit in a bar. I'll be a man and you'll be another man fifteen years older. And then I'll carve another face on the back of your head.

The Spanish woman sat up straight. If you talk to Bachir like that, I don't wonder he hits you. He's just apologized to you.

Why does he hit somebody smaller than he is? That's cowardly. And why doesn't he just sleep with women? Boys are not to sleep with anyway.

What's that? said the old Spanish woman. But Bachir began to talk at the same moment.

I know, he said. I'm sorry, Abdeslam. I know I've been rough with you, but from now on I'm going to stop the games. You'll see.

You swear? said Abdeslam.

I swear.

22

What Bachir had just said made Abdeslam feel much better. He went to his room and shut the door. Then he sat on the bed smoking kif and listening to the laughter in the next room. After a while he decided to set up his train and start his animals running. He wanted to see if he could arrange them so that the rabbit could knock the bear on to the track just before the train came along. He ran out into the middle room and brought out the toys.

The rabbit and the bear knocked each other over, and the train went on around the track. He set them up again, putting the rabbit nearer the bear. While the others were talking Bachir came over to him.

I saw Aouicha today, he said.

Abdeslam stopped playing and turned to look at Bachir. You did? I haven't seen her in three days now.

I wonder why she hasn't been around, Bachir said.

I don't know.

She told me she might come by tonight.

Bachir, said Abdeslam. Where does Aouicha live?

A few streets below here. Not far. Why?

She's never invited me to see her.

Bachir stared at him. You don't want to go there. She doesn't want you there.

How do you know where she wants me? Abdeslam demanded.

I'm telling you not to go, that's all.

How can I go? said Abdeslam. I don't even know where it is.

Bachir walked away without answering.

The Spanish woman was drunk and laughing very loud. Hola, gazelle! she cried. Come and sit here, I want to talk to you.

When he went over and stood near her she said to him : Why don't you come and live with me? She leaned her head to one side and almost shut her eyes as she looked at him. I have a beautiful little girl at home. You should see her! I'll introduce you to her and when you grow up maybe you two could get married. What do you think of that?

The woman's words made Abdeslam suspect that she was laughing at him, but since she looked at him very seriously as she spoke, he could not be sure.

That's very kind of you, señora, he said. Thank you. But I'm a Moslem, and I couldn't ever marry a Nazarene. Besides, I don't want anybody telling me what I've got to do. I used to live with my family, you see, and I come from a very big family. I've got relatives everywhere. But thank you anyway, señora.

Shortly afterwards there were three quick knocks at the door : Tantantan! Abdeslam jumped up and ran to open it. Aouicha was standing there.

Aouicha! he cried, not looking at her face.

She came in. How are you? she asked him.

Fine.

Aouicha greeted the others. Then she took off her haïk and handed it to Abdeslam.

I'm sorry I couldn't come to see you, she told him. I was so busy. Two families of relatives came in from the country and stayed at my mother's house. And I had to be there to help her. The house was full of people.

Hamdoul'lah! I hope they were all in good health, said Abdeslam.

Thank you, she said.

The others were talking and laughing. Aouicha pulled Abdeslam into a corner. And Bachir? she said. Has he been all right with you?

Abdeslam looked down at the floor. Now that Aouicha was here with him, and acting as though nothing at all had happened between them, he felt much better about her. Bachir, he said, slowly. Yes, we get on fine together. But some day I'm going to drink his blood.

She seized him by the shoulder. What has he done?

He's hit me and knocked me down and cursed me. He says if I don't go into his room and sleep with him in his bed, he's going to beat me up and drag me there.

I knew it would come sooner or later, she said. She walked over to where Bachir was sitting and stood looking down at him.

Bachir! she cried. Why did you hit Abdeslam? If I'd known what was going to happen I wouldn't have gone to my mother's. I'd have stayed here the whole time.

Bachir frowned. Stay out of it, he said. It's got nothing to do with you. What I do in this house with the boy is my business. To me you're just a whore off the street. All you need to worry about is how much money you can earn out there.

Aouicha was silent for a moment. The others stopped

talking. You're right, said Aouicha. I've always had to think about money. Especially when I was with you. I wonder how many times I watched you open my handbag and take it all, so you could eat and pay your rent. But I'm just a whore off the street! All I can say to that is, at least I'm in the street! Filth like you gets flushed down the sewer. They don't leave it in the street.

Look, Aouicha, said Bachir. You're asking for two beautiful slaps, one coming and one going. They'll be right along if you don't shut your mouth.

Ya bastante! cried the old Spanish woman. Bachir! We don't want to listen to your squabbles. We want to dance and sing.

She began to clap her hands and tap her feet, and soon she was singing a flamenco song. Then she got up from the couch and pulled her dress off over her head. She threw it across the room on to a hassock and sat down again in her underwear, fanning herself.

Abdeslam stared at her. Why did you take your dress off? he demanded.

It's hot! she said.

But you're sitting in front of us with all your flesh showing. Nobody else is hot.

Yes, but you see, I'm stout.

No, you're not. You're just old. That's why your flesh is all shrivelled and wrinkled like that.

You should never say such things! You're a very rude boy!

But you shouldn't take your clothes off, Abdeslam told her. There are four men looking at you, and you're sitting in your underpants. That's not the custom here. Nazarenes can only do things like that in their own countries in Europe. Here when a woman sits in the same room with men, she has to keep her clothes on. It doesn't matter how

hot she is. She can always go and get some fresh air somewhere. But she can't take her clothes off.

The woman did not answer. She looked at him angrily.

Aouicha was doubled over laughing, and Bachir's
friends laughed too. Bachir said : Shut up, Abdeslam, will
you?

Yes, I will, he said. I'll shut up and you can all get
drunker. The señora's going to have one more drink, and
then she's going to take off the rest of her clothes.

The old Spanish woman jumped up and put her dress
back on. It's very late. I've got to go, she told them. She
was still in a bad humour.

I was only joking, Abdeslam told her, trying to stop her.
Stay and dance for us, please.

She pushed past him and went out. Bachir did not seem
to notice that she had gone.

23

Thursdays and Sundays were the busiest days of the week for Abdeslam. The city was full of Djebala who came in from the country to spend the day selling and buying in the market. All day the café was full of men in djellabas and turbans. They even filled the tables on the pavement outside, and Abdeslam ran without stopping between the fire and the tables, carrying tea and coffee and Coca-Cola. Most of the customers smoked kif, and many of them tried to sell it to him. He never bought any, because when he refused he had found that they gave it to him anyway. His kif box was always full on these days. And they constantly passed him their pipes to smoke, so that by the time Si Mokhtar arrived in the afternoon to count the money, Abdeslam's head would be about to burst from the pressure of the kif inside it. Sometimes when he got back to the mahal he would have sharp pains in his head and he would be unable to focus his eyes properly. He would go straight to his room, drop on to the mattress and fall asleep. Some nights Bachir came home for dinner. He would go in and wake Abdeslam so that they could eat together. Otherwise Abdeslam would sleep until Aouicha came to knock later in the evening.

One afternoon Aouicha did not go to the nylon factory to work. She stayed at home until about the time when Bachir usually got back from the port, and then she set out for the mahal. When she got there Bachir had just arrived.

Where's Abdeslam? she asked him.

He's in his room asleep.

She walked into the bedroom, with Bachir following behind, and together they stood looking down at Abdeslam as he slept. After a moment she turned to Bachir and said : If you touch him you'll wish you hadn't. Remember, I'm just a whore off the street.

Bachir smiled. He put his finger to his lips and pulled her back into the middle room.

That's all over with. Can't you forget it? I was just teasing him. I didn't know he'd think I was serious.

I know, I know, said Aouicha.

What do you mean, you know?

I know you. You think I believe you?

I tell you I'm not going to touch him! he shouted. And why should it make any difference to you? He's no use to you anyway. You told me that yourself a long time ago. He's not ready yet, you said.

Aouicha laughed and put her hands over her face. She had not told Bachir about the night she had spent with Abdeslam. What she was thinking about now was the way in which Abdeslam had changed since that night. He always seemed glad to see her, yet she felt that he was constantly watching her, the way you watch someone you think may be a thief. And he found fault with her all the time. He would quote long sections of the Koran to her, so that she could not interrupt or contradict. Then when he had gone on for such a long time that she was no longer listening, he would quickly begin telling her again what was wrong with her, before she had a chance to say anything. This did not make her love him less. It only meant that she could not get near him.

But remember, she told Bachir, if you do, you'll wish you hadn't.

Someone coughed. They glanced up and saw Abdeslam in the doorway looking at them.

What's the matter? he wanted to know. Why are you both standing there like that?

We're just talking, said Aouicha. But she was wondering when he had woken up and how much he had heard.

Can't we have some tea, Aouicha?

Of course, Abdeslam.

Bachir was annoyed. He had hoped Abdeslam would go on sleeping for a while longer. You've got two hands, he told him. Make it yourself, if you want tea. Aouicha and I are talking.

You're all against me, Abdeslam said. You never want what I want.

Why should we? said Bachir. What do we care what you want? You're only a boy. Why should anybody wait on you? Are you sick?

No, but I'm tired. It's a hard life working in the café.

Bachir burst out laughing. You think you're having a hard life? Here? You should have seen my life. Then you'd know what the world is about. My father died when I was five. Just my mother and my brother and I. Then she died when I was twelve, and we two boys were alone in the house. And then even he died. I went through much worse than you.

Abdeslam was making his tea. It's impossible, he said.

Your father was dead. Mine was alive, and he threw me out.

I know, but at least you studied first. You can read Arabic, and I can't read anything. What chance did I ever have?

You never would have learned anything anyway, Abdeslam told him. That's the kind of man you are

When he had made the tea Abdeslam sat down on the divan with his kif pipe and smoked as he drank it. Soon he was imagining that he was the captain of a ship. The crew had mutinied, and he stood alone high on the bridge facing them all while the ship sped over the sea. In the evening when he smoked, the kif often made him think he was someone else living another life.

Later, after they had eaten, he got up. My feet hurt tonight, he said. I've been running back and forth all day, carrying tea to the Djebala. We've never had so many customers.

You should be glad, said Bachir. You make some money that way.

I am glad. But I'm going to bed, he said.

I think I'll go out for a while, said Bachir.

Don't you want me to massage your feet a little? Aouicha asked Abdeslam.

No thanks, he said quickly. You'd better go when Bachir goes. I'm tired.

I'll come tomorrow when I leave work, she told him.

He turned to her. Aouicha, you always come here to see me. You've never asked me to go and see you. I don't even know where you live.

I have nowhere to invite you to, here in the city, she said. Just one small room, and it's dark. You wouldn't like the place.

Yes, I would. I'd like to see it.

Some day I'll invite you to my house and you can meet my mother. She lives in Aïn Hayani.

That's not far, said Abdeslam.

Yes, but she's very busy. I can't just go any time and take you.

I want to see where you live in the Medina, he insisted.

Maybe some day, she said. Then he thought he saw her glance at Bachir, and Bachir glance at her, as if they had some secret between them.

Some day! Some day, he said to Aouicha. I know what that means. That's what they say when they mean never.

He stared at the floor. You're all against me, that's all.

You're crazy, said Bachir.

I'm going to bed. Good night.

24

One morning not long afterwards when Abdeslam woke up his feet were very sore. They had been hurting for several days, but not enough to make him think about it. This day they hurt badly. He went to work at the café. Si Mokhtar saw that he was limping as he worked. What happened to you? he said.

I have pains in my feet.

How'd you get pains in your feet?

I don't know.

He worked that day as well as he could. The next day was harder. By the time afternoon came he could not stand up without touching the wall. He asked one of the customers to fetch Si Mokhtar from his house in the Casbah. When Si Mokhtar arrived he sent Abdeslam home.

Abdeslam went to bed. Bachir came back from work and saw him lying there. Now what? he said.

My feet hurt.

Bachir pulled off the blankets and looked at his feet. They're swollen, he said.

It's not the first time, said Abdeslam. I used to go bare-foot when I was little.

They're very red too, Bachir said.

There was a knock at the door. It was Aouicha. She came in and looked around. Where's Abdeslam? she asked.

In there in bed. He's sick.

They went into Abdeslam's room. We're going to soak your feet in hot water, said Bachir. They'll feel better in the morning, you'll see.

They brought a bucket of hot water and made him sit up with his feet in it. But in the morning they were even more swollen and red. He lay in bed all morning, until finally Aouicha arrived.

How are you?

Worse.

I don't know what to do for you, she said.

You can't do anything. They just hurt. They hurt a lot.

Don't you want some breakfast?

All I want is for my feet to stop aching. He pulled the sheet up over his head and cried.

Aouicha watched him a while and began to cry too. I wish I had the pain instead of you, she told him.

That's impossible, he said.

About five o'clock in the afternoon the skin on his feet began to split open and water came out. When Bachir got home and saw him he said: I'm going to get my cousin who works at the British hospital. He'll know what to do.

Bachir went out and called the hospital. It took him a long time to get hold of his cousin. When he finally reached him at the other end of the line he asked him to come to his mahal later in the evening and look at Abdeslam's feet. But his cousin said he was working at night and could not leave the hospital.

I'll send an ambulance for him and they can look at him here, his cousin said.

Bachir went back to the mahal to wait. A little while later two interns arrived with a stretcher. They put Abdeslam on it and carried him out through the alleys, with many people watching along the way, to the Zoco Chico. There they slid him into the ambulance and set out for the hospital on the Marshan, Bachir and Aouicha sitting inside with him.

At the hospital they carried Abdeslam into the doctor's consulting-room and put him on a long table. Soon the doctor came. He was English, but he spoke Arabic.

What's wrong with this boy?

Bachir was standing there. He said : His feet are covered with big blisters and the water's coming out.

The doctor examined his feet. You're all right, my boy. There's nothing the matter at all.

All I want is for them to stop hurting, Abdeslam told him.

I'll give you a nice injection and then we'll put you into a clean bed and give you something to eat, and then you'll feel good. And you'll go to sleep and we'll see how you are in the morning.

They carried him off to bed and an English lady came and put a needle into his thigh and rubbed his skin afterwards. Soon he felt no more pain.

Bachir was standing by the bed. He'll have to stay here? he asked the doctor.

Yes.

How long?

A few days. Until his feet are healed.

How much will it cost? Bachir asked.

I'll need a deposit of ten thousand francs, said the doctor.

I haven't got that with me.

You can leave a part of it and bring the rest later.

Aouicha opened her purse and took out the money. Here it is, all of it, she said. The doctor took the notes and gave her a receipt, and Bachir and Aouicha went out. Abdeslam was left behind in the room.

There were five beds. One was empty. The other three beds had Moslems in them. They began to ask Abdeslam questions. What's the matter, boy? Why did they bring you? How do you feel?

My feet, he said.

One of the men said : I have a bad foot too. It's my eyes, said another. With me it's my stomach, the last one said.

It's just the soles of my feet, Abdeslam said. He liked hearing the words. They made the trouble seem further away. I'm only going to be here a few days. The doctor said I was all right.

One of the men was looking at magazines, another was lying back singing a song, and the other was playing cards. Abdeslam looked around the room. Each bed had a small table beside it, and each table had a pitcher of water and a glass on it, and a towel hanging from a rack at its side.

On the wall opposite there were two pictures of the hospital's Messiah. He was wearing a burnous from the Sahara over his shoulders and a Berber turban on his head. Underneath each picture there were words printed in Arabic letters.

That's strange, Abdeslam thought when he read them. So many words written there about Allah, and not one about Mohammed. But these people are Messihiyine. They laugh at Allah and they want everybody to be like them and do what they do.

I see you're looking at the pictures, said one of the men. What do you think of them?

They're all right.

Can you read Arabic? he asked Abdeslam.

Yes.

And what does it say there underneath?

Abdeslam began to read all the words aloud. When he had finished he asked the others: Did you understand anything?

Yes, they said, not sounding very sure. Some of it. Not all.

You understand the words about Allah, said Abdeslam. And the words you didn't understand were the words of Satan. Has there ever been such a man as the Messiah?

He's right. That's the truth, the men said. The Koran says there never was and never will be.

The door opened and the doctor came in. He began to speak with Abdeslam. Now you're with us, we're going to take care of your feet, and tomorrow the nurses will come and take you outside to sit in the garden. And soon you'll be well and strong.

Incha' Allah, said Abdeslam. If I'm still alive.

Oh, we mustn't say such things. Now, you look to me like a boy who loves Allah very much. The doctor winked at him.

Of course I love Allah. How could anybody not love Allah?

People who love Allah want to live, said the doctor. We don't want to hear any talk in our hospital about dying. Now you're going to eat something, and then you're going to sleep.

Abdeslam lay there, thinking of how Aouicha had paid for his bed in the hospital. He could not be sure what he felt about her, however, because he did not understand her. She had gone on being friendly with Bachir after Bachir had called her a whore in front of his friends. This seemed very strange.

A nurse brought in the supper. It was served in dishes made of aluminium. Abdeslam was surprised. Like jail! he exclaimed. The men laughed. The food had no flavour to it. They ate brown beans and cold fried fish and salad. Afterwards they had sliced bananas and then coffee.

Abdeslam was annoyed because Bachir had not let him bring his kif and pipe with him. One of the men finally offered him a cigarette of black tobacco. When he had smoked it he said good night to the others and went to sleep.

In the morning, before breakfast, the doctor came in. Good morning to all of you, he said. And they all said: Good morning.

Have you forgotten? That's not the way we say good morning in the hospital. Here we say: Good morning, and good morning to the Messiah.

Then the men said: Good morning, and good morning to the Messaih.

And you, Abdeslam? I didn't hear you say anything. But maybe your voice is so small it got lost.

How can I say good morning to somebody I can't even see?

You're a stubborn boy, Abdeslam. But you'll change, said the doctor. Now I'm going to tell you all a story. Once there was a man who had lost his eyesight. He was blind. He came here to the hospital, this poor man, and we examined his eyes. They were good, but he could not see with them. We told him we were not going to operate on him. We were simply going to give him some drops and a book about the Messiah. We gave them to him and he took them home. Each night he put the drops into his eyes, and then he put the book under his pillow and went to sleep. One night he dreamed that a man dressed all in white came to him and placed his hands over his eyes. And in the morning he could see perfectly and he said: Thanks to Allah, and thanks to the Messiah who gave me back my sight.

When Abdeslam heard this he said: But doctor, if there were people in the world who could put their hands over blind people's eyes and make them see, they'd do it, and cure them, and there wouldn't be any blind people left. And the streets are full of blind people.

There's only one who can do that, Abdeslam, and that is the Messiah.

But no Moslem can understand who the Messiah is! Abdeslam cried. Moslems only know Mohammed and the nbia. We don't understand anything else. We know that if a person is sick and gets well, it's not the doctor who saves him. It's Allah. The doctor only helps. And if Allah wants to send you a disease that no doctor can cure, there's nothing anybody can do about it.

That's true, of course, said the doctor. Well! It seems to me that for one small boy you have a great deal to say. He looked at Abdeslam quickly and went out of the room. A little later a nurse came in and gave him an injection of medicine. She put another kind of medicine on his feet. Finally they brought in the breakfast.

When the four of them had eaten and the nurse had taken away the dishes, the doctor's wife came in and began to listen to each man's heart and breathing. She sat on each bed and listened to each man. Then she came to Abdeslam and told him to take off his pyjama-top. And she tapped him and listened and made him turn over and tapped his back and listened.

The doctor said there's nothing the matter with me, he

told her. I had to come, because where I live I'm all alone.

What? she exclaimed. Don't you live with your family?

No.

But why is that?

He explained to her. Then he said : I like to study my own language and my own religion, and that's all.

Of course. Everybody should study the subjects he likes, she said. But you should go and live with your parents. Don't you go home to see them now and then?

No! Never. I can't.

You poor boy. I feel so sorry for you. Now lie back and rest. I've got to go.

A little while later Aouicha arrived to pay him a visit. She sat down on a chair by the foot of his bed. Before she had a chance to say anything he asked her : Did you bring any kif?

You can't smoke kif in the hospital, she whispered.

I've got to have some kif.

I've brought you six packets of cigarettes. Look! she said. She pulled them out of her bag. Then she took out two cans of pineapple, two bars of chocolate and two boxes of matches. While she was sitting there talking to Abdeslam Si Mokhtar came in. He walked over to the bed, kissed Abdeslam on the forehead and sat down looking very sad.

What's the matter, Si Mokhtar?

I'm sorry to see you sick, that's all. I hope Allah will make you well and give you a long life, my son.

Thank you, Si Mokhtar.

The men lying in the other bed were listening. The doctor came in. Abdeslam, he said.

What, doctor?

I wish I knew what makes you so stubborn and ungrateful. You don't seem to understand anything anyone says to you.

But what am I supposed to understand? Abdeslam asked him.

That's the very thing I mean, the doctor said. You don't even know that.

I don't want you to be angry, Abdeslam told the doctor. But if you do get angry, I'll be angry too. Because I came to this hospital to rest and get well. And it costs money to stay here. I'm here and I want to get well, that's all. I'm a Moslem. That's why I'm stubborn and don't understand anything anybody says to me. Moslems are stupid.

I said nothing about Moslems! I never talk about Islam, said the doctor. I don't know anything about that.

No one can know anything about Islam, said Abdeslam. Allah can kill either of us in the next minute if he wants. But he doesn't come down into the city and walk through the streets looking for blind people so he can put his hands in front of their eyes and make them see. Like the blind man you spoke about, who put the book under his pillow. Who could ever believe such a story?

I believe it, said the doctor angrily. The man was a Cherif.

A Cherif?

Yes, indeed.

That doesn't mean anything. I'm a Cherif too.

You?

Of course. Both my father and mother are Chorfa.

That's very nice, the doctor said.

An old English nurse came into the room. The doctor took her arm and brought her over to Abdeslam's bed.

This boy, he said. You should hear him talk.

I've heard him, she said. You'll just have to be patient. I think he's a very good boy underneath.

126

She looked at Abdeslam and smiled.

Yes, I'm sure he is, said the doctor.

Aouicha and Si Mokhtar stood up. They said good-bye and went back to the Medina. That was the only time anyone came to visit him. He stayed another four days in the hospital.

The day before he left they let him get out of bed. He still limped, but he could walk much better than before. When the afternoon came for him to leave he said good-bye to all the interns and nurses.

The doctor was in the waiting-room reading his Messiah book to the people who wanted to see him. The nurses sent Abdeslam in to wait with them, because he had to get a chit from the doctor before he could go home. He waited and waited and he began to feel cold.

The doctor was saying to the people : We are here in this hospital for one reason. To cure people of illness. But all these medicines that we give the sick people are good only because there is somebody helping us. Now, who is that person, the one who helps us every minute of the day, who is always beside us when we are curing people of their sickness? No one can see him, but we know that person is the Messiah.

And he went on in this way. Abdeslam was very tired of waiting. Finally he raised his hand and waved it, as if he were back in school.

May I say something, doctor?

The doctor did not look pleased, but he said : Yes, you may. What is it?

You're a doctor.

Yes.

And you're curing people who are sick. And you say someone is helping you. I can tell you who is helping you. It's Allah.

The other Moslems who sat waiting nodded their heads.

It's Allah, and everyone knows it's Allah. People come here because they want to get well. When they come in they find that they have to listen to you talk first, and so they say yes. But when they get well, they know the Messiah had nothing to do with it. Only very ignorant people from the mountains could ever believe what you say. Can't I go home soon? I've been waiting a long time.

The doctor merely looked at him. Finally he said : Yes, you may go.

Abdeslam stood up, still talking. Country people might, but city people who've studied the Koran, never !

If you've finished, Abdeslam, I want to say that you've got to come back tomorrow for your medicine. Here, take this note and bring it with you when you come.

Abdeslam walked up to the platform where the doctor sat, and took the note. Then he strode down the aisle between the benches to the door.

Make an earring of your Messiah, he said under his breath as he went out. If I'd known the Messiah lived here I wouldn't have come. I'd have gone to the Spanish Hospital where Jesucristo lives. He did fine things too. He made bread and brought dead people back to life.

He continued to mutter as he went down the steps and through the garden. And he looked around to see if anyone was following him, but nobody was. There was no one waiting for him at the gate either, because no one knew he was leaving the hospital that day. He limped down the avenue towards the Medina.

25

Abdeslam was so tired when he got back to the mahal that he lay down on his bed and fell asleep for an hour or so. When he awoke he went to look for his kif pipe. He found it in the middle room on a shelf beside his box of kif, and the box still had kif in it from the other day. He sat down on the divan and began to smoke. It was such a long time since he had smoked that the first half-dozen or so pipes went straight to his head, and this made him begin to think about his life. It seemed to him that if people only knew how bad his life was, someone would come from somewhere to help him. He told himself that it would be impossible for them to know how he was living and then forget him.

After a while, when it grew dark, he got up and went into his room. The kif was making him feel very heavy, and he heard a roar like the sea in the back of his head. He wanted to stretch out on his bed.

As he lay there looking upwards with his hands folded over his chest like a dead man, he lost track of time as it went by, and he forgot where he was. The lamp in the room was very dim. It flickered. He watched the shadows moving up and down in one dark corner of the room, and it seemed to him that the figure of a man was growing clearer on the wall. He kept watching, his heart beating very fast. And a man was there, dressed all in black, with a black cape and a black turban, and a black veil over the lower part of his face. His eyes were very large and dark and when Abdeslam stared into them he saw fire deep inside.

The man began to walk towards him until finally he stood beside the bed. Slowly he pulled out a black hand-kerchief and waved it above Abdeslam's head, scattering drops of water that were as cold as ice over his face and neck. Then he started to back away, and Abdeslam had to get up and walk after him. The man backed through the middle room and into Bachir's room. Then he rose into the air, floated backwards over Bachir's bed and was sucked into the wall above the headboard.

At this moment Abdeslam found that he too was floating towards Bachir's bed, and then he saw that he was lying in it. And two very small children wearing djellabas came in and stood by the bed. When he looked at them he could not see their feet or their hands or their faces—only their djellabas. They both climbed up on to the bed and sat down at the edge, and they began to talk together. Their voices were exactly alike, so that they sounded like the same voice, but he could not understand what either one was saying. Soon they jumped down to the floor and stood stiffly by the head of the bed, and then they exploded in puffs of air.

Abdeslam opened his eyes and found that he was not in Bachir's bed at all, but in his own. He sighed deeply and felt better. Then he heard knocking on the door. Tac,

tac, tac, tac, tac. He jumped up and ran to let Bachir in.

What time is it? Abdeslam asked him.

Six thirty.

I've been sitting around here going crazy for three hours, Abdeslam told him. I saw things in front of my eyes, things I've never seen before.

Bachir put a fresh bottle of wine on the taifor and sat down. What sort of things? he said, pouring himself a glass.

Abdeslam sat down facing him and lighted his kif pipe. I was just sitting here, he said. And my brain began to work all by itself like a machine. Then I got tired of thinking and went and lay on my bed. Then something bad happened.

He told him about the man who had come out of the corner, and how he had followed him into Bachir's room and seen him disappear into the wall.

It's the kif you smoke, said Bachir, shaking his head.

I don't know about the man, said Abdeslam thoughtfully. But I think the two little boys were angels. They came to tell me something, only I couldn't understand them.

Bachir set his wine-glass down on the taifor with a bang. I'm telling you, Abdeslam, the kif's going to get into your brain. It's going to ruin your health, and in the end it'll kill you.

I was still looking at them when you knocked on the door, Abdeslam went on.

Listen, said Bachir. Kif makes everybody afraid. That's why you thought you saw all those things.

No, Bachir. Those two angels went away when you knocked because you had that bottle of wine with you. They knew a Nazarene had come, and so they left. They didn't want to be in the house with an unbeliever.

Bachir laughed and reached out with the glass towards Abdeslam. Here, have a drink, he said. You need it.

Abdeslam paid no attention to him. Kif doesn't drive you crazy or kill you. Only Allah can do that. You don't know anything, Bachir. Why do you try to talk?

Bachir looked at him. There are just the two of us here now, you little whelp. I'd like to break your back.

It's the wine that's talking, not you, said Abdeslam. It's not your fault. That's what alcohol does to a man. He curses at everybody, falls down in the street, breaks everything, vomits everywhere, gets his face smashed in and goes to jail. That's the life of a Moslem who drinks.

Bachir laughed. And kif doesn't ruin the health?

No. Kif keeps you quiet. You don't want to fight or argue. Maybe you just want to sit and listen to music or watch the clouds go by, or just think.

You're crazy, said Bachir. I've smoked more kif than you've ever seen, and it never did anything like that to me. Nobody smokes kif except people who think it's a thousand years ago.

Abdeslam pointed his finger at Bachir. You're twenty-nine and I'm thirteen. How can you look at me and tell me I ought to drink? Do you think a Moslem man should keep telling a Moslem boy to drink? That's why I say it would be better if you didn't talk.

I won't offer you any more wine, said Bachir. Or beer or brandy. Will that make you happy?

It'll be a lot better, Abdeslam said.

Aouicha arrived a little later and they had dinner. Then they sat back to drink tea and Aouicha began to complain.

I don't know why I go on day after day feeling so sad, she said. I don't know what's the matter with me.

There's nothing the matter with you. You're just nervous, Bachir told her.

Maybe you've done something bad, said Abdeslam. Have you?

Aouicha laughed. No.

Try and remember, he said.

She was silent a moment. No. I haven't done anything, she said.

That's impossible! If you'd never done anything bad in your life you couldn't feel sad.

She looked at him, startled. I suppose that's true, she said.

Of course it's true. Tell me something bad you did once. Please.

It's nothing, said Aouicha. But I remember once when I was a girl I went out to the country with a lot of other girls, and one of them was a lot stronger than I was and she kept pushing me around and yelling at me. And later I left them all playing and went off by myself, and I found a big pile of rocks that the workmen had left beside the road. I was angry and I pushed the pile so the rocks would roll down. And suddenly a big snake came out, and I ran. I waited a while and then I went back to the pile of rocks. The snake was gone, but I found ten little eggs there under the rock where it had been. And I took them and kept them in my pocket with my hand over them. And when we were ready to have lunch I hid behind some bushes and broke all the eggs into a bowl and scrambled them, and then I poured soup over them and stirred it all up and gave it to the girl I didn't like. And she drank it. When we got back to town she had awful pains in her stomach. And in the morning when she woke up her belly was all puffed out. I went over to her house to see her and she was in bed. I asked her what was the matter and she said she didn't know, but she felt very heavy and she couldn't speak very easily. She said her tongue wouldn't move. It was hard to understand what she said. She said she couldn't tell whether she was lying down or standing up. She didn't even feel that she was there at all. And she was sweating and she said she was cold. Her voice was different from the way it had been before. After a while I could hardly believe she was the same girl, she had changed so, and I began to cry. She reached out and took my hand and then she cried too. And she smiled at me and said: I'm sorry I was so mean to you yesterday.

Aouicha paused. I got up and went out. I couldn't sit there with her any longer. The next day they told me she was dead. I wanted so much to tell her the truth and ask her to forgive me. But she was dead.

She stopped talking. Then Abdeslam said: You see? I was right. That was a terrible thing you did. Excuse me a minute.

He got up and went into his room. There he got out the Koran and sat down on his bed to look through it for the passage he wanted. When he found it he went back into the other room with the open book in his hand.

I've found what I was looking for, he told them. It says that Allah can forgive a person who commits a crime, but only if that person lives the way he should afterwards. Allah loves people because they were his idea. He likes to play with them and watch what they do, and so he lets them go on living and pardons them while they're alive. Then he punishes them after they die. So if he doesn't punish you now, he'll do it later. That's all.

I know. It was an awful thing to do, she said. But I don't think that's why I'm sad so often. I just wake up sad and feeling nervous. Sometimes I can't even sleep, because I'm afraid I'll see terrible things in front of my eyes if I do.

Abdeslam was going to say something, but Bachir, who

134

was now very drunk, began to sing. Yes! You killed one girl. But I'm going to kill everybody! Everybody!

Aouicha paid no attention to him. Of course, she said, when I did that to the girl, it was long ago, before you were born, I think.

She went on talking. A few minutes later Bachir toppled over and his head hit the divan. A bottle tipped on its side and all the wine spilled out on to the mat. Bachir lay with his head on the divan and his buttocks in the pool of wine. They tried to rouse him, but he could not hear them talking to him or feel them tugging at him.

Abdeslam let Aouicha out and bolted the door after her.

26

The next day Abdeslam was kept very busy in the café. In the afternoon a drunken American with a beard came in, ordered a glass of black coffee, and when he had drunk it, wanted to pay three pesetas instead of three pesetas fifty for it. Abdeslam told him the price was always three fifty, but he would not believe it. Some other customers finally put the American out into the street.

Si Mokhtar came, counted the cash and gave Abdeslam his share.

Thank you, Si Mokhtar, he said. I've been thinking a lot and I'd like to ask you a favour.

What's that? said Si Mokhtar.

I've been thinking there are two kinds of people in the world, day people and night people, and they're not the same. I'm tired of seeing day people all the time. I want to see the others. I'd like to work here at night for a while, if you'll let me.

No, no! Certainly not! Night work in this café is very rough, Si Mokhtar told him. You're not old enough to do it. A lot of drunks might come in at two or three in the morning and make terrible trouble. You wouldn't be able to handle them.

But you could stay here with me a few nights and show me how, and afterwards I could stay by myself.

No, no. I couldn't leave you alone here at night.

But why not, Si Mokhtar?

I can't let you do it, that's all. I'd be too worried, and something would be bound to happen. No, no, no!

Abdeslam was angry. He said good-bye and went out.

There was no one in the mahal. He sat down and smoked a few pipes of kif.

It was not long before Bachir arrived. Oh, you're here, he said.

What have we got for dinner tonight? said Abdeslam.

Kifta, peas and eggs, said Bachir. And wine.

Ayayay! Wine, food and whores. That's your life. Abdeslam looked at Bachir with disgust.

You know, Abdeslam, the last few days you've been getting on my nerves again, Bachir told him. You're not a fqih. You're just a boy like any other boy, and you can't go around telling other people what to do and what not to do.

That's not true, said Abdeslam. I'm not like anyone else. You don't know. Even if I live to be thirty I'll never be like anybody else, because I'm different.

Bachir laughed.

I am! Abdeslam insisted. My mother only kept me seven months inside her instead of nine. And when I was born I had a bag around me. And I stayed in a box full of cotton in the hospital. And when they sent me home to my mother I only weighed six pounds. And the whole family and all the neighbours said : That baby can never live, or if it does, there'll be something the matter with it. But

I'm still alive and my brain works just as fast as anybody else's. The only thing is, I get nervous.

One of these days I'm going to break your kif pipe over that shaved head of yours, Bachir told him. That would be the best thing anybody could do for you.

That's right, said Abdeslam. And the best thing for you would be if I smashed all your bottles. You're just an old drunk.

Bachir picked up an egg and tossed it at Abdeslam's head. It broke and ran down his face. This made Bachir laugh. To him it was a joke, but Abdeslam did not understand. He seized his glass of tea and hurled it at Bachir. It hit the wall.

You don't know how to take a joke, Bachir told him. Look at you, getting all excited over an egg.

Abdeslam went to the sink and washed his face.

27

Life went on, sometimes quietly for three or four days, sometimes with quarrels which never went beyond words. When Bachir was alone with Abdeslam he was usually sober and pleasant. But when friends came in and he got drunk with them, he would begin to find fault with Abdeslam. Several times Abdeslam tried to explain things to the guests. He told them that Bachir shouted at him because he always wanted Abdeslam to sleep with him, and that each time he said no, Bachir would get angry all over again. But when they heard this they laughed a great deal, and he thought they did not believe him.

One afternoon Abdeslam took a walk through the quarter. He wanted to see streets he had never seen before, and so he went along passageways and into alleys that had no way out except the way he had gone in. All at once he saw Aouicha ahead of him at the far end of a long passageway. He was in the dark, in a place where the houses made a tunnel, and he knew she had not seen him. He went quickly into a side-alley and hid in a doorway. Soon Aouicha came by and disappeared around the corner into another narrow street. Abdeslam ran to the corner and watched. A young man came out of a doorway on the left, crossed the street and joined her. They hurried into a building on the right, and he saw no more of them.

He took good note of the building and the street and continued his walk, very unhappy. It had never occurred to him that Aouicha might have a lover and he felt that she had betrayed him.

That's where she lives, he thought. And that's why she won't take me there.

He began to walk in the alleys of that neighbourhood, always watching out for Aouicha in the fear that she might see him first, before he had time to hide and guess why he was there.

It seemed to him that Aouicha had noticed the difference in his feeling towards her and was suspicious of him. She did not come so often to the mahal, and when she did come she stayed only a little while and always left if Bachir came in. Abdeslam thought about it, and each day he felt more bitter. He had taken it for granted that Aouicha loved him, and it hurt him to think that each night she had been going home to the young man. More than anything he was angry with her for the night when Bachir had stayed on the mountain and she and Abdeslam had slept together naked. She had played with him and laughed at him because he did not know anything. He was sure that she had gone home and told the young man and that they had laughed together about it.

Another day he saw Aouicha when he was wandering in her neighbourhood. She was standing in the doorway of a house in a street not far from her own. Abdeslam went into a tobacco-shop and began to ask for several brands of cigarettes he knew the man did not have. Every few seconds he went to the door and peered out. Then he saw Bachir coming along. When he reached Aouicha he walked past her as if he had not seen her. She began to follow him at some distance behind, and they went around the corner. Abdeslam waited an instant and then went out into the street, keeping them both in sight ahead of him. They arrived at Aouicha's street and turned into it. He began to run, and got to the corner in time to see them both go into the building where she had taken the young man.

Now Abdeslam found himself walking very fast without any idea of where he was going. His heart was beating with great force and he breathed heavily. If Bachir went to Aouicha's room, it could only be to go to bed with her. He understood that Aouicha did not even have a lover. She's just a whore from the street, he thought, remembering what Bachir had said.

To calm himself, he walked all the way out to the Charf and climbed up to the empty mosque on top. He stayed until the sun went down, looking at the city below, and then he went home.

The first thing Abdeslam did when he got to the mahal was to wash himself with two pails of cold water. Then he put his clothes back on and got ready to go out for another walk. At the last minute he decided he would rather stay in. He made himself some tea and sat down to smoke his pipe. He had been thinking of Aouicha and Bachir all afternoon, but now he was thinking only of Bachir. With the hatred he felt for him, and the kif in his brain, he began to believe that Bachir hated him just as much. There was no way of knowing when Bachir would attack him.

The only way is to be ready to hit him first. I've got to

keep thinking until I find some way, something to do it with.

He began to search in his mind for a small weapon which could always be there in the house ready to use, but which Bachir would not notice.

He knocked me down, he thought. A man who's worth nothing in the world. All he knows is how to work in the port and get drunk in the kitchen and shit in the latrine.

Bachir came in that evening with a Negro who carried a guinbri. This is Embarek, he told Abdeslam. He lives down the street.

Bachir poured the man a glass of brandy.

No thanks, not for me. I only smoke kif.

Abdeslam quickly filled his pipe and passed it to the Negro. When the man had smoked he filled it with his own kif and gave it back to Abdeslam. Then he picked up his guinbri and began to pluck the strings, and soon he sang some Gnaoua songs. Abdeslam listened very carefully because the man was a professional musician. When he stopped singing Abdeslam told him how much he had enjoyed it.

Soon a young man arrived. As Bachir showed him into the middle room Abdeslam got up and went into his room so that he would not have to meet him. He smoked a few pipes sitting on his bed, hearing the three men talking together. Then someone else knocked and Bachir went to open the door. He heard Aouicha's voice and frowned, because he did not want to see her. Finally he was too bored to sit alone any longer. He got up and went back into the other room.

The Gnaoui was sitting in the same place and Aouicha sat beside him. On the other side of her was the young man. Aouicha was laughing with the men, and she only waved at Abdeslam.

Come and sit here, the Gnaoui told him. Abdeslam stood in front of him but did not sit down.

The Gnaoui went on speaking in a low voice. Why are you living in this house? You shouldn't be. You look like a bright boy. Sit down. Here, beside me.

No, said Abdeslam. I'm all right, thank you.

The Gnaoui shrugged, took up his guinbri again and started to play, and the young man got up and danced. Bachir watched him for a while and then he too jumped up and danced opposite the young man. Each one had a glass in his hand and they drank as they danced. Abdeslam and the Gnaoui went on smoking kif, and Aouicha merely sat and laughed.

Soon Bachir stopped and drew Abdeslam aside. He pointed at the young man who was still dancing. That boy's name is Mimoun. He used to come and see me once in a while. He likes brandy.

That's none of my business, Abdeslam said. He can drink brandy or wine or water with you. It doesn't matter to me. I don't know him. He's your friend, not mine. Binatskoum.

You don't have to talk like that.

I didn't say anything. I just said it's your business, not mine. Why shouldn't he come and spend the whole night if he wants to?

Mimoun was listening. He came over to where they stood.

I see this new boy you've got hasn't learned how to talk yet, Bachir. Can't you teach him?

Shut up, said Bachir.

I'm not going to hit him, said Mimoun. He's just a baby.

Hit me or don't hit me, said Abdeslam. Whatever you like.

The boy's got a nasty temper, Bachir said.

Why do you always start to argue when your friends are here? said Abdeslam. Drink your brandy and your wine, and sing and dance. That's what you're here for.

Yes, and you're here to keep your mouth shut, Mimoun told him. Your pants are still full of shit.

Abdeslam laughed. Suddenly he felt that he was a famous criminal, the kind of criminal for whom people have great respect, because they know that even when he seems to be doing nothing he is watching, always waiting for the moment to act. He looked at Mimoun and said : You'll pay in blood, my friend. The others heard and paid no attention.

A quarter of an hour later, when they were all singing and laughing again and everyone had forgotten about the quarrel, Abdeslam got up quietly and started out of the room.

Where are you going? asked Aouicha.

Just to the latrine, he told her.

He went into the room and shut the door. On the floor was an empty half-litre bottle. He picked it up, filled it with water and replaced the cork. Then he went back into the middle room holding the bottle behind him by its neck. He walked over to where they were all sitting and passed behind Aouicha. Mimoun was sitting bent over, talking to the Gnaoui. Abdeslam brought the bottle down on top of his head. The bottle exploded like a bomb. Mimoun stood up, and then fell over on to the floor and lay there.

Aouicha screamed. They all sprang up. What have you done? You've killed him! What's the matter with you?

They were bending over Mimoun. He's all right.

Abdeslam began to laugh. I told him he'd pay me back

in blood. You see the blood coming out of his head? Now I feel good.

Mimoun opened his eyes. You hit me, he said.

Aouicha brought soap and water and iodine for Mimoun. When they had finished cleaning him Bachir said to Abdeslam : Now kiss the top of Mimoun's head.

Abdeslam did not want to, but he knew that everyone would be against him if he refused, so he did it, making a face when he felt the hair against his lips. Then Bachir made Mimoun kiss the top of Abdeslam's head.

Now you're friends again, he said.

Mimoun did not stay much longer. After he was gone Abdeslam said to Bachir : You saw something new tonight. You saw what a boy can do to a man.

Yes. I saw what you did to a friend of mine, said Bachir. I invited him here to my house.

Yes, and I know why you invited him, Abdeslam told him. So he'd get into a fight with me and beat me up and nobody would put the blame on you.

The kif makes you see everything upside-down, Bachir told him. How can anyone talk to you?

I don't ever do you any harm, Abdeslam went on. We could live together all right if you'd just leave me alone. Only you're a drunk. You're no good.

All right, all right, said Bachir. I'm no good, I'm a drunk, I'm a criminal, whatever you like. Only shut up! Shut up for once and go to bed!

Good, said Abdeslam. He got up, went into his room and bolted the door. He sat down on the bed and cupped his chin in his hand, thinking of the insult he had just taken from Bachir. There must be something, he said to himself, I've got to find something. A knife is no good. I need something I can hide in my hand, something small that doesn't look as if it could hurt him. If it doesn't kill him it can change his face so that every time he sees himself he'll remember me. That's what I want.

At last he went to bed. Even then he lay there for a long time, still searching his mind for the right thing to use on Bachir.

28

The next day Abdeslam went early to the café and told Si Mokhtar that he was not going to work any more during the day.

If I can't work at night, I don't want to work at all, he said. He did not say that this was so he could be out of the house at night, when Bachir was there.

I told you, nights are bad. Something would happen for certain.

I can do it, said Abdeslam. Nothing will happen.

All right. If you want to see what it's like, you can stay and help me tonight. That way you'll know how hard it is.

Abdeslam was happy. Can you give me some kif? he said. I haven't got any.

Si Mokhtar measured him out three matchboxfuls and Abdeslam walked up to the boulevard. It was a bright day and there were many tourists sitting in the cafés. He looked into the shop-windows. Finally he went into a store and bought a pair of black shoes. Then he went down through the Zoco de Fuera to the stalls at Bab Fahs. There was a knife here which he looked at for a long time. It opened when you pushed a button and made a clicking sound. He did not buy it because he did not have enough money.

Soon he was walking along the Avenida de España under the palm trees. On one side the waves were breaking across the beach, and on the other people sat at the tables along the pavement. It was too windy to sit anywhere and smoke kif and so he decided to go back to the mahal.

He put his new shoes on the shelf in his room, had lunch and lay down for a long siesta.

About seven o'clock he went to the café. He was very eager to see what would happen. Si Mokhtar said he was going to stay by the fire and make the tea and coffee, while Abdeslam served the customers.

It was about midnight when Si Mokhtar said to Abdeslam: Watch those four who just came in.

They were drunk. Abdeslam went to their table. Seeing him, one of them called out to Si Mokhtar: I see you've got a waiter now.

Yes, Abdeslam said. He's got a waiter. What will you have?

The men all ordered black coffee. As Abdeslam served it to them he noticed that there were two very rough-looking men standing outside the door. It seemed to him that they were hatching a plot out there.

These are real night people, aren't they? he said to Si Mokhtar.

Wait, said Si Mokhtar.

They sat together for a while by the fire. Soon there was much shouting outside in the street.

What's that? said Abdeslam.

When Si Mokhtar saw that the man who was shouting was coming into the café he said: You stay here by the fire. I'll go and see what he wants.

No, said Abdeslam. Let me try.

The man coming in tipped over two chairs and sat down heavily on a bench alongside the wall. Abdeslam walked over to him, paying no attention to the chairs, and said : *Salaam aleikoum.*

Since the man did not answer, Abdeslam finished the greeting for him, saying : *Aleikoum salaam.*

The man looked up and began to laugh. How's that? You said *salaam aleikoum* and then answered yourself!

Of course, said Abdeslam. I always do that when I'm talking to the wall.

The man laughed harder. You're pure sugar, he told Abdeslam.

Thank you. What would you like to drink?

I'd like a Coca-Cola, the man said.

When Abdeslam took him the bottle the man told him to get another and sit down with him.

They sat drinking Coca-Cola. After a bit Abdeslam pulled out his pipe and offered it to the man.

No, I don't smoke kif. I don't even smoke cigarettes. The only thing I like is alcohol.

Tell me. Each time you start to drink, what does it feel like? Abdeslam asked him.

It's wonderful! You forget the things you hate. When things get too bad you have to forget them. Then everything is good again.

Of course, said Abdeslam. Because before you start to drink you're thinking of something real, and it makes you nervous because you know it's real. So you get drunk and you begin to think upside-down. Then you feel good.

The man looked at him as if he had not understood. How much do I owe you? he said.

Abdeslam told him and he paid.

I'll see you again, he said as he started out.

Please, friend, I want to ask you something, Abdeslam told him.

What?

These two chairs you tipped over. Couldn't you please pick them up before you go?

All right, said the man. He set the two chairs upright and went out.

The four drunks who had come in earlier all had their heads on the table, sleeping. Abdeslam went over to them and woke them up. Excuse me, he said, your coffee's getting cold.

Let it get cold, said one of the men.

Why don't you drink it and pay for it, and go home and sleep? How are you going to sleep like this? There's no room. It's only a café. It's not a hotel or a pension. You can get tea, coffee, Coca-Cola, orange crush, whatever you like. But there's nowhere to sleep.

The men raised their heads. That's right, they said. There's nowhere.

They finished their coffee and paid for it. Then they went out into the street. Si Mokhtar and Abdeslam were alone in the café for the moment.

Bravo! cried Si Mokhtar. I've never seen anything like it! The way he put the chairs back. If I'd asked him, he'd have broken them both over my head. And he paid for your Coca-Cola. Half the time he doesn't even want to pay for his own. I can't talk to him about it either. He goes crazy.

Oh, you know him? said Abdeslam.

Of course. He's an old friend from years ago. But I can't talk to him when he's drunk.

He must have paid for you lots of times, said Abdeslam.

Oh, yes. He's a good man.

So it doesn't matter so much if he won't pay now and then, does it?

Si Mokhtar laughed.

When morning came Si Mokhtar gave Abdeslam a hundred and sixty-five pesetas, and Abdeslam went home to bed.

29

Abdeslam woke up about the time the sun was setting. When he opened his door to go and wash he found Bachir sitting with Aouicha and two men. He waved to them as he went through the room, but he wished the house had been empty.

While he was washing Aouicha made him some café con leche, and two fried eggs, which he ate with bread and butter. Then he went and sat with the others, taking a second glass of coffee with him to drink while he smoked his kif pipe.

How did last night go? Bachir asked him.

There wasn't as much trouble in the café last night as there was here the night before.

Do you still hate me tonight?

What difference does it make? Abdeslam asked him.

The taller of Bachir's two friends looked at Abdeslam and frowned. What's the matter with you? he demanded. Bachir only asked you a question.

Abdeslam looked at him angrily. Bachir hates me. He's

always hated me, he said. So why does he ask me if I hate him?

You don't know what you're saying, said Bachir.

Yes, I do, said Abdeslam. My father drew blood when he hit me. And so did you. I can't get blood back from him. But some day I'll get it from you.

Stop it Abdeslam! said Aouicha. Nobody wants to hear such things, especially from a young boy.

You shut up! cried Abdeslam, jumping up and glaring down at her. You haven't got anything to say. You're a woman. You're outside the whole thing.

He ran out of the house, leaving the door open.

At the café he found Si Mokhtar sitting with his head in his hands. He had a fever. Abdeslam sat down by him.

I'm dying, my boy, he said.

No, no! cried Abdeslam. You're just sick, that's all.

I'm going to shut the place up and go home to bed. You go home too.

No. I'll stay here and run the café.

Si Mokhtar was feeling so ill that he said : All right.

Abdeslam was happy. Customers came in all evening long, and he served them and everything went very well. The men played cards and dominoes and parchesi, and drank their tea and smoked their kif. By half past two there were only three men left in the café. They were regular customers who came in each night and sat for an hour or two.

Soon three other men walked in. They ordered Coca-Cola and he served them. Then he saw one of them take out a bottle of Coñac Centenario and begin to pour it into the glasses of Coca-Cola.

I'm sorry, said Abdeslam. It's forbidden to drink alcohol here. Please put the cork back in and hide the bottle. This café has no licence for that.

The man pouring the brandy looked at him and smiled.

Why don't you come to my mahal and stay the night with us? he asked Abdeslam. We'll put the bottle away now and all four of us will go to my place and drink it together.

I'd go with you, Abdeslam said, except that I can't leave the café.

I see. Tomorrow night, then?

Why don't you take your friends home and come back by yourself later? said Abdeslam. You haven't got enough brandy for four anyway.

The other said this was a good idea and in a little while they paid and went out. Abdeslam imagined that the man would soon be so drunk that he would forget everything. But a little after four o'clock in the morning he came back. He was drunker than he had been earlier.

Here I am, he told Abdeslam. Let's go.

Wait for me outside. I'll be out in a minute.

The man seized him by the arm. No! I came to get you and I'm going to take you. Now.

He tried to push Abdeslam towards the door. Abdeslam struggled and the customers jumped up and made the man let go. Then they threw him outside into the street.

In the morning Si Mokhtar did not appear. I wonder if he's dead, Abdeslam thought. He decided to wait and see what would happen. He waited all morning. At eleven o'clock a small boy came running in and said to him: Si Mokhtar says to shut the café and go home.

All right. Tell him as soon as I've shut it I'll be up to see him.

The boy went away.

Abdeslam did not close the café. He sent out for some lunch and stayed on, serving the customers. It was about four in the afternoon. As he stood by the fire he looked up and saw Aouicha in the doorway. He went over to her.

You worked all night, and now you're working all day, she said. You look very tired. Your eyes are almost shut.

He did not want to tell Aouicha that he knew about her and Bachir. In spite of that he said bitterly : I suppose Bachir sent you.

I bought you something today, she told him, as if he had said nothing at all.

Abdeslam handed her his key.

Take it to the mahal, he said. Si Mokhtar wants me to close the café, but I've got to keep it open. I need the money. I'm going to stay here until I find somebody to take my place.

Aouicha went away.

At six in the evening the drunk who had been thrown out the night before came into the café looking angry. He was sober now. He pointed to his jacket, which was ripped.

I want to know why those men jumped on me here last night, he said.

You don't know why? said Abdeslam.

No, I don't.

What did you say to me last night?

Nothing. I invited you to my mahal, that's all.

They don't like to hear that kind of talk here.

But I was drunk.

It's all right, said Abdeslam. Nobody got hurt.

At that moment four men came in and greeted the man. He sat down with them and forgot about Abdeslam.

Abdeslam went on working, but he had begun to feel very heavy and tired. As he stood by the fire pumping the bellows Bachir arrived.

What do you think you're doing? he demanded. Working all night and all day, and now all night again?

I can't shut the café. Si Mokhtar always leaves somebody to look after it when he goes home.

Don't you know any of these men who are sitting here? There must be one of them who knows how to make tea. Get him to stay while you come home and sleep a little.

I'll see, said Abdeslam.

If I'm not back in a few minutes with something for you to eat, Aouicha'll bring it later.

Abdeslam watched Bachir go out. It seemed very strange that they should still be thinking about him and bringing him food. They don't know I found out, he told himself. They think everything's still the same.

At ten o'clock Aouicha arrived with his dinner. He got it from her at the door, since she could not enter the café. Eat it with appetite, she told him, and he thanked her. After she had gone, and while Abdeslam was still eating, Hadj Mohammed, an old friend of Si Mokhtar's, came in.

Where's Si Mokhtar?

Abdeslam told him.

At the end of his story he said: And I haven't slept yet.

Hadj Mohammed offered to tend the café for a while so that Abdeslam could sleep a little. Abdeslam sat down in one chair and put his feet up on another. In an instant he was asleep. He slept until half past five in the morning, and would not have woken up then if there had not been a racket outside in the street. He got up and looked out of the door. A few drunken youths were fighting among themselves. He turned to Hadj Mohammed and said: I slept a long time.

I didn't want to wake you up, Hadj Mohammed told him.

Soon Abdeslam went out and bought the milk and

pastries for the café. Hadj Mohammed had put aside the money he had taken in during the night, so that it would not get mixed up with the money in the cash-box. When Abdeslam got back he gave him the money and the list of sales. Abdeslam checked it and thanked him and they had breakfast together. Afterwards they smoked kif and talked.

Hadj Mohammed left, and Abdeslam stayed on in the café working. He felt certain he would have news of Si Mokhtar during the morning, but none came.

Early in the afternoon Aouicha came to the door and stood there shaking her head. You're still here? she said.

He shrugged. What can I do?

I'm going to bring you some lunch, she told him.

Much later Hadj Mohammed appeared and sat down. Abdeslam was about to go over and ask him for news when he saw Aouicha in the doorway with his lunch. He took the pots from her and said good-bye to her. Then he asked Hadj Mohammed to have lunch with him. He had no news of Si Mokhtar. While they ate he began to ask Abdeslam all sorts of questions about his family and his life.

Why are you here working in this café? he wanted to know.

I had some trouble, said Abdeslam, and I couldn't stay at home any more. But I'm all right, thanks to Allah.

It's a bad place for you to be, said Hadj Mohammed. Don't make friends with any of the men who come here.

I don't, said Abdeslam.

It was already dusk when Si Mokhtar walked in. He had been to see a fqih and they scarcely recognized him. He usually wore European clothes, but this evening he was dressed in a djellaba with a white turban around his head, and he wore very wide Algerian trousers.

I'm much better, he said. But Abdeslam, you look yellow. You must be very tired.

No, said Abdeslam. He could not admit it was true.

He wouldn't shut the place, Hadj Mohammed was saying. He wanted to go on working, because he said you never left it alone. He's a funny boy. He told me he was studying the differences between day customers and night customers!

Si Mokhtar laughed. Well, my son, what do you think of the night people? How did you like being with them?

I didn't like it, Abdeslam admitted. They're all right, I suppose, but there's something the matter with them. They're like bats. They'd bump into the wall if they went out in daytime.

You're right! said Si Mokhtar. I didn't think you'd like them.

You ought to go home and rest, said Abdeslam.

I'm working tonight, and you're the one who's going home to sleep, said Si Mokhtar. And you'd better sleep for two or three days, from the way you look. You're very pale.

Abdeslam gave Si Mokhtar the accounts, and Si Mokhtar handed him four hundred and twenty-five pesetas.

That's more than half, Abdeslam told him.

I told you, go on home, said Si Mokhtar.

Abdeslam thanked him and left.

30

When Abdeslam got to the mahal he knocked. Aouicha still had his key. She opened the door and let him in. She was busy frying raif on the brazier. He did not speak to her.

He went into the latrine and washed his hands and face and feet. Then he walked into the middle room and sat down. On the taifor in front of him was a large glass bowl full of fruit. Aouicha came in drying her hands.

Where did that come from? he said, pointing at the bowl.

That's what I bought for you.

Thank you.

There were oranges, apples, a few pears and bananas, and two lemons, a large shiny one and a small discoloured one.

You must be terribly tired, Aouicha said.

I'm not tired.

Would you like some coffee? It's hot.

Yes. Give me a glass.

He took it and thanked her.

Aouicha!

What?

Can you get me a razor-blade? I want to cut a corn off my toe.

Aouicha got up and went into Bachir's room. She came back unwrapping a new blade and handed it to him.

Thanks. He laid it on the taifor and lighted his kif pipe. Now and then he took a sip of coffee. Finally he picked up the razor-blade and began to cut off the hard part of the flesh on his toe. He went on cutting until he had taken it all off. When he finished he lit a match and held it under his foot, burning the parts where he had cut off the skin.

What are you doing? Aouicha cried. Why are you burning your foot? You're the craziest boy I've ever seen.

It doesn't hurt. And besides, it kills the germs.

He laid the razor-blade on the floor beside him, picked up all the pieces of hard skin and went to throw them down the latrine. As he came out and shut the door behind him he said: Aouicha.

Yes?

If I were sixteen, do you think Bachir could beat me in a fight?

No, I don't think he could, she said.

Abdeslam sat down again.

If you eat lots of fruit you'll get strong, she told him. It's very healthy.

That apple looks good. He reached for a large red apple, and at the same time he took the two lemons out of the bowl.

Lemons don't belong with fruit, he told Aouicha.

Why not?

Because all the other fruit is sweet and you can bite into it. But lemons are sour. You need a kilo of sugar.

Lemons are perfectly good fruit, she said. And they look pretty in the bowl. They're such a bright yellow.

Abdeslam laughed and looked at her. Yes, there are people like that too. Pretty to look at and sour inside.

Yes, yes, I know, she said impatiently.

Abdeslam set the apple on the taifor and began to smoke. As he smoked he thought of Bachir. Aouicha sat quietly without speaking. And he went on refilling his pipe and smoking it until the kif boiled in his head. He could think of nothing but Bachir, and the thoughts rushed through his head so fast that he had to get out of their way. He picked up the razor-blade and then he picked up the shiny lemon and began to make small cuts in the side of it. The smell of the rind was very strong.

Why are you spoiling the lemon like that? demanded Aouicha.

You can get a kilo for two pesetas, he told her without looking up.

Aouicha did not speak again and Abdeslam went on making little gashes in the side of the lemon. Then he tried to push the blade farther into its flesh. It went in, but when he tried to cut the lemon in half the blade would not move, and instead sliced into the end of his finger. The blood dripped on to the lemon.

The lemon's not yellow now, he said. It's red.

Aouicha cried out. Ay! What have you done?

Nothing. He went into the latrine and let the cold water run over his left hand. In his right hand he held the lemon with the razor-blade still embedded in its rind. Soon the blood was no longer coming out of his finger. He turned off the tap and stood up, rubbing the lemon across a wash-rag that hung from a hook on the wall

Where the lemon had touched the cloth, the cloth was cut.

Ah! said Abdeslam. He moved the lemon along the rag once again, and again it cut.

He stood still for a moment and then he went back into the middle room. Aouicha had iodine ready to put on his finger.

He pulled the blade out of the lemon and threw the lemon into the garbage-pail. He took the blade into the latrine and dropped it through the hole in the floor. He sat down again and went on thinking. This time he thought only about lemons.

31

That night Bachir came in sober. I see you've made raif, he said to Aouicha. To Abdeslam he said : What happened to your hand?

I broke a glass in the café, said Abdeslam.

Aouicha looked at him with surprise, but she did not say anything.

Hasn't Zohra come yet? asked Bachir.

I didn't know she was coming, Aouicha said.

Bachir sat down and they had the raif with their tea. While they were eating Zohra knocked at the door.

Msalkheir! How are you? How have you been? She sat down with them.

A few minutes later there was another knock. Go and open the door, Bachir told Abdeslam.

You open it. Whoever it is, it's going to be a friend of yours, not a friend of mine.

Bachir got up and opened the door. A man came in carrying a basket which he handed to Bachir. Then he greeted the others and sat down. Abdeslam had seen him before. They called him Charlot because he had big feet.

Meanwhile Bachir was looking into the basket. There were three bottles of Coñac Fundador on top. He took them out first, and then some fried fish, some olives stuffed with chiles and a loaf of brown bread. He quickly opened one of the bottles and poured himself some brandy. He drank it in one gulp.

The blood of Jesucristo, said Abdeslam, watching him.

Then Bachir rolled some olives in a piece of bread and began to eat. He turned to Abdeslam and said as he chewed : I know. And the bread and olives are Jesucristo's flesh. Isn't that right, Charlot?

After they had finished the first bottle Bachir opened the second. Then Charlot jumped up and ran out to the bacal. He brought back a case of Coca-Cola and they began drinking brandy and Coca-Cola. When the second bottle was half empty Bachir turned suddenly to Abdeslam and looked at him as if he had never seen him before. Finally he said : You're so beautiful, Abdeslam, now you've got some hair again.

Abdeslam looked back at him, and he looked at Aouicha, and at each one of them in turn. Then he said : Thank you, Bachir. You're beautiful too. And Aouicha's beautiful, and Zohra.

Zohra's a gazelle ! Bachir said, pinching her thigh. She's got a wonderful big pair of buttocks back there.

Zohra stared at Bachir coldly. Yes, I know, she said.

You're going to like it tonight, Zohra. You hear?

You can't, with me, Bachir. Never.

Don't say never to me. When a woman's in bed with me she does what I want, front or back.

That's terrible ! said Abdeslam. You have no shame at all, Bachir. You're like some criminal.

Please, Abdeslam, said Aouicha. It's no use. Don't start arguing with Bachir again.

Bachir would not let go of Zohra. Tonight you're going to stay with me. And you're going to do everything I want you to do.

I'm not! she cried. Let go of me! She pulled away from him and went to sit on the other side of the room. You're right, Abdeslam, he's a criminal. It's a shame they leave him alive.

He's already half-dead, Abdeslam told her. Let him drink his brandy and go on dying.

That's enough, that's enough, Charlot said. I've got to be going. He got up. Don't get drunk! he told Bachir.

When he had gone, Bachir said : I'm going to take Zohra to bed now.

Zohra said nothing.

Do you want to go home? Abdeslam asked her.

I can't, it's too late.

She's staying with me! Bachir roared.

Abdeslam went on talking to Zohra. Why don't you and Aouicha both sleep in my room?

Bachir suddenly stood up and began to sway in front of them, and they all quickly got to their feet. He staggered towards Zohra and seized her arm. She shoved him violently with both hands and he stepped backwards against the divan and lost his balance. As he fell he struck his head on the wall.

The two women went into Abdeslam's room and got into his bed. When Abdeslam thought they were asleep he went in and turned out the light. Then he lay down on the mat and covered himself with a blanket.

He had almost fallen asleep when he heard Zohra whispering. I'm afraid! she kept saying. He's going to wake up and break down the door and kill all three of us!

Don't be afraid. Go to sleep, Abdeslam told her. He won't get up. You can go to sleep and not worry.

Yes. Lie still and go to sleep, Aouicha told her.

32

In the morning Aouicha looked into the other room. Bachir had already gone to work. She went back into the bedroom and woke up Zohra and Abdeslam. Then she made coffee. Abdeslam did not want any. He went to a café in the Zoco Chico for breakfast. All that day he sat around the mahal smoking kif and thinking about Bachir.

When evening came Bachir appeared for a few minutes while he got ready to go out and eat with friends. Aouicha came and prepared supper for Abdeslam. After the two of them had eaten they went to the cinema.

It was a film about gangsters and Abdeslam watched closely. Did you see how he came in through the window and stuck the knife into the man's chest? he whispered to Aouicha. That was good. They're professionals, these men.

Just look and keep quiet, she said.

He looked. The film showed much more about how to rob and kill people. At midnight it was over and they went home. Bachir was in his room asleep.

They sat down in Abdeslam's room.

I can still see that man coming in through the window with the knife, said Abdeslam. He was quiet a while. I feel a little sick, he said.

You do? You ought to go to bed.

He waited again before he said: Killing Bachir like that would be like getting rid of a scorpion. Everybody'd be glad.

Oh Abdeslam! Stop talking nonsense! Aouicha told him.

I really do feel sick, he said. I want to go to bed.

If you're sick, I'm going to stay right here, she said.

With Bachir, he thought. In his bed.

He got up and went into his room. He turned out the lamp, undressed and got into bed. Soon he heard Aouicha begin to snore lightly. He merely lay there thinking and he found himself crying there in the dark. I've got what I need now, he thought, and something bad's going to happen. But once it's happened I won't cry any more.

He got up and lighted the lamp. Then he sat down on the edge of his bed and began to smoke. He sat there for a very long time, filling his head with kif.

Much later Aouicha opened the door and peered in. What are you doing? she whispered.

Smoking, he said.

The mouddin is calling the fjer, she told him. It's five o'clock in the morning.

I haven't slept yet and I'm not sleepy.

But why not? She came inside and shut the door.

I don't know.

You're still thinking about that film, she said. It scared you. That's what's the matter.

Yes, he said, I'm afraid.

They heard Bachir get up and wash and they stopped

talking. But he had already noticed their voices and he called out : The day's yours, and the night too. Don't you ever sleep, you two?

It's your fault! called out Abdeslam.

Bachir slammed the door as he went out.

Why do you blame him? said Aouicha. He's got nothing to do with it.

And your fault too, he added.

Mine! Why?

I'm sick of you both! he cried. I don't want to see either of you any more!

Abdeslam!

I'm only a boy, I know, he went on. And that's why I don't need a thirty-year-old woman around all the time.

I never heard such things! she cried. What's the matter with you, Abdeslam?

You know how to open a door and shut it, he said. That's all you have to do. I want to sleep.

He got into his bed and turned towards the wall.

She stood looking down at him. Wouldn't you like me to get in with you? she whispered.

Please, he said, just leave me alone. I need to get some sleep. I'll sleep better if there's nobody in my room.

She was shaking her head. It's the kif, she murmured. Bachir was right, it's rotting your brain.

He sat up suddenly and screamed at her. The kif's not rotting my brain! It's you! You're rotting my brain! Get out and don't come back!

Aouicha put on her haïk and went out, slamming the door even harder than Bachir.

She can cry or die or do whatever she likes, he thought, lying down once again. He fell asleep and slept until half past three in the afternoon. Then he got up and washed and went out to the café.

Si Mokhtar greeted him. How are you this fine day?

I need a glass of coffee, Abdeslam told him.

Si Mokhtar made the coffee and gave it to him. Did you get a good sleep? he asked him.

No, said Abdeslam. I still haven't really slept. Just a little.

You don't look very well, Si Mokhtar said.

I'm all right.

Si Mokhtar filled his pipe and gave it to Abdeslam. I have an idea you're still worried about Bachir.

Yes, you're right.

He's no good. I know him. He's not worth worrying about.

I know him too, said Abdeslam. Everybody knows he's no good.

You shouldn't talk to him when he's drunk. Leave him alone.

Why don't you smoke and fill the pipe again for me? said Abdeslam. I've still only had one pipe.

Si Mokhtar filled the pipe and gave it to him. You ought to come and live with me and my wife and get out of that place, he said. Maybe some time you'll really do that.

Abdeslam knew he never would, but he could not say so. Tell me, Si Mokhtar, he said. I want to ask you something.

What's that?

Which is the best brand of razor-blades? The sharpest?

Razor-blades? What do you care about razor-blades? You don't have to shave yet.

I just wondered which kind shaved the fastest.

Well, I think Sevillanas are the best, said Si Mokhtar. But I don't understand.

I don't have to shave now, said Abdeslam. But some

day I will. And I won't have to ask anybody which brand to buy.

Si Mokhtar laughed. Abdeslam handed him the pipe.

A little before the end of the afternoon Abdeslam left the café. On the way home he stopped at a bacal and bought a kilo of lemons and two packets of Sevillana razor-blades. When he got to the mahal he went into his room and bolted the door. He sliced two lemons in half and squeezed the juice into a glass. He added sugar and water and set the glass on the taifor with his kif pipe and his mottoui, and the bag of lemons and the two packs of razor-blades. Then he sat down in front of the taifor and smoked a pipe of kif.

Presently he opened a packet of razor-blades. He took a good-sized lemon and stuck four blades into it at equal distances from each other. Then, holding it by the two ends, he threw it as hard as he could against the door. It hit and fell to the floor. When he went over to see what had happened he found splinters of one of the blades embedded in the wood.

Then he heard someone come into the house. Quickly he put the razor-blades and the lemon away.

People were talking in the middle room. He opened the door. Bachir was there with some friends and the taifor was covered with bottles of wine. He decided to have dinner at a restaurant. It would be worth the money not to have to eat in the mahal. He called out Hello! as he went through the room and walked out into the alley.

He sat eating for a long time in a small restaurant in the Saqqaya. He was thinking about his life and he kept telling himself that the time had come to do something. He could not live any longer with Bachir in the mahal. He felt that if he stayed on there he would become like Bachir. The idea made him feel very sick.

When he had finished he was suddenly sleepy. He got up and paid and walked through the windy alleys to the mahal. There was no one there. He went into his room, bolted his door and undressed. The wind rattled the blinds. He got into bed. After he had lain there for a while listening he blew out the lamp.

33

Abdeslam got up in the morning feeling sad and not knowing why. He washed, put on his clothes and started out to the café for breakfast. On the way he stopped at a stall to buy ten pesetas' worth of churros. He went into the Calle del Comercio with a large bagful of them. Some small boys were playing in the middle of the street. One of them saw the pastries he was carrying. Give me one! he cried, and he began to run along beside Abdeslam.

Here, said Abdeslam, and he handed him a pastry. Then all the boys came and swarmed around him, begging for churros. He gave one to each and went on to the café.

Good morning! said Si Mokhtar.

Can you make me a glass of coffee fast? Or let me make it myself?

What's wrong, Abdeslam? Are you upset? Or did you have too much kif last night?

Nothing's wrong, Si Mokhtar. I just feel as if something is going to happen. Something bad.

You should move out of that place, said Si Mokhtar. Then you could forget about Bachir . You could just leave him there in his filth.

You know, Si Mokhtar, said Abdeslam, if only I were a little older, sixteen or seventeen, I could get rid of all these hoodlums that bother you at night. I could do it without any help too.

Si Mokhtar smiled. I wouldn't want to see you try it, he told him. Don't get that into your head. It would be the end of you.

Maybe, said Abdeslam. But he did not believe Si Mokhtar was right, because he thought that with a lemon in his hand he could do what he wanted to anyone.

It could be the end of me, he said. I know I'm not going to live long anyway.

Don't talk that way, boy, said Si Mokhtar.

I'm not! And I wouldn't believe anybody who told me I was. What time is it?

Si Mokhtar looked at his watch. Half past eleven, he said. Why don't you mind the café a while for me, and I'll go home and get some lunch and bring it back here for us? At least you got some sleep last night. I can see that. But I don't want you to come back to work until tomorrow night. You've got to get another night's sleep.

All right, said Abdeslam, and Si Mokhtar went out.

A few minutes later two men came into the café and ordered two teas. Abdeslam merely sat smoking his pipe, looking at them. After a moment they called out again.

Two glasses of tea!

Abdeslam said : The café's shut.

What do you mean, it's shut? It's open.

The man's not here, he said. He did not feel like getting up and going to the fire.

Why didn't you say so? They looked at each other and

one of them said : The boy's half-witted. They walked out.

At half past one Si Mokhtar came back with the food. Abdeslam sat just as he had left him, but his eyes were shut.

Abdeslam! he shouted.

What?

Are you hungry?

A little.

Let's eat then. He spread out the food. There was a big tajine and a loaf of brown bread. Afterwards Abdeslam made two glasses of green tea and they smoked while they drank it.

In the middle of the afternoon Bachir appeared in the doorway and beckoned to Abdeslam. What do you want? Abdeslam shouted. It had begun to rain and he did not want to go outside.

Bachir came in and stood just inside the door, speaking in a low voice to Abdeslam. Look, I need two hundred pesetas. I've got some friends at the mahal and I want to buy a lot of stuff.

Abdeslam said : Of course. He took out two hundred pesetas and handed them to Bachir. Bachir thanked him. and left.

What did he say? asked Si Mokhtar.

He wanted to borrow money, so he could get drunk.

And you gave it to him? Why didn't you tell him your wallet was empty?

I want him to think he can rely on me, said Abdeslam.

What do you mean, rely on you?

Si Mokhtar, if you have a dog in your house and you always feed him bread and water, and I come along and start giving him meat, your dog is going to follow me home and stay with me. And he's going to forget you. Isn't that right?

Yes, son, that's natural. Bread and water's not the same as meat.

That's why I gave Bachir two hundred pesetas. I want him to have confidence in me. He's a dog.

Here. Take the pipe, said Si Mokhtar.

Abdeslam had dinner at a small restaurant around the corner and went back to the café to sit with Si Mokhtar and smoke. They talked and laughed and made tea and coffee for the customers. Finally Si Mokhtar said to Abdeslam : I can't understand what interests you in that house, or why you want to go on living there with Bachir. You know what kind of man he is.

As long as he doesn't bother me I don't mind being there, said Abdeslam. He got up. I'm going back to the mahal to see what's going on there.

What do you care what's going on? It'll just be a lot of drunks sitting around the same as always, Si Mokhtar said. He hoped to persuade Abdeslam to stay where he was.

Abdeslam went out without answering.

When he unlocked the door of the mahal he heard singing.

Salaam aleikoum.

Aleikoum salaam.

Bachir was sitting with two men and a girl. Abdeslam had never seen any of them before. He stared at them and they stared at him, surprised to see a small boy suddenly appear.

Bachir was drunk, but he seemed to be in a good humour. How are you? he said several times to Abdeslam.

Abdeslam sat down. He took out his pipe and smoked for a time, watching. Then one of Bachir's guests said to him : Fill me a pipe, will you? I didn't bring mine with me.

Abdeslam filled his pipe and gave it to the man. When he got it back Bachir called to him: Now I want it! Fill it up! And Abdeslam passed it to him. He did not give it back after he had smoked, but borrowed his friend's mottoui and smoked several pipes. Then he filled it again and gave it back to Abdeslam. Here. Take it, my diamond, he told him.

Abdeslam took the pipe without answering.

Bachir picked up a bottle and began to drink from its neck with a gurgling sound. The girl turned to him: Why don't you drink out of a glass like a human being?

Bachir set the bottle on the floor beside him and belched. Now the girl began to look at Abdeslam. What's he doing in here? she said angrily. Get him out of here. I don't like children sitting around watching me.

Bachir was about to speak, but Abdeslam interrupted him. I was just wondering the same thing about you, he told her. What are you doing here?

What do you mean? she cried. I'm a woman and I'm sitting with men. You're a child and you've got no business to be here.

I know, he said. You're one of the women who sit with men. The kind of woman who likes the smell of money.

Shut up, Abdeslam! said Bachir. Go and play with your train or something. Haddouj, take that darbouka and hit it, because I'm going to get up and dance a hole in the floor.

She lifted up the drum and began to beat it, and Bachir danced. The dance went on and on and Bachir seemed to get more drunk as he danced. Suddenly he tripped over Abdeslam.

Abdeslam tried to help him up, but Bachir wrapped his arms around him and began to kiss him on the lips and he could not get away.

177

The two men and the girl laughed at Abdeslam's struggles. Finally Bachir relaxed his grip a bit, and Abdeslam pushed him away.

Bachir went and sat down. He called over to Abdeslam. That was all I wanted, he said, and smiled at him.

That's nothing, said Abdeslam. We're friends, after all. He filled his pipe and passed it to Bachir. Here. Smoke, he told him, and he gave him his mottoui as well. Help yourself, he said. Then he got up, went into his room and bolted the door.

He took off the sweater he was wearing and put on a jacket instead. He picked up a lemon from the pile of them on the shelf and stood looking down at it. He shut his eyes tight and the tears ran out.

He's kissed me in front of his friends, he was thinking. They all think I'm his wife now.

He unwrapped two razor-blades and inserted them side by side, close together, deep in the lemon's rind, so that he could hold the fruit easily in his hand. Then he set it down and packed his clothes into his suitcase. He kept out a large handkerchief, which he wrapped around the lemon before putting it into the pocket of his jacket. There was some water in a pail in the corner of the room and he washed his face so that no one would see that he had been crying. Then he went out and sat down again with Bachir and his friends.

Where have you been? said one of the men.

I had a little too much kif, he told him, and I wanted to wash my face and cool off.

Bachir was lying opposite him on the floor. His mouth was open and saliva was running down his chin. Abdeslam looked at him. Bachir ought to mend the roof, he said. It's raining on his face.

You're the smart kind, aren't you? said Haddouj, looking at Abdeslam in a way he did not like. You know everything, don't you?

So you've noticed that? he said. I didn't think you could tell the difference.

She turned to Bachir angrily and nudged him, trying to make him open his eyes. Can't you get him out of here? she cried.

Bachir sat up. Yes, he said to Haddouj, laughing. He needs to be put to bed, so he can study his lesson. I'm going to teach him something new tonight.

Why not? said Abdeslam, without looking at him. After your friends have gone home.

Bachir glanced at him in surprise. What was that? he said.

Of course, Abdeslam said quietly. After they go.

Bachir looked puzzled, but he said : Good!

Abdeslam smoked four or five more pipes while the others went on drinking. Soon Haddouj had hung both her breasts outside her dress. She looked very drunk.

Abdeslam stared at her. If there were ten more whores like you, he told her, the whole country would be rotten.

Look at who's talking, she said scornfully, pointing her finger at him.

Only the rottenest whores hang their breasts out like that. And you're one of them.

If I weren't Bachir's guest I'd break a few of those bottles on that smart little head ! she shouted.

Bachir seemed to be asleep again. The next time anyone thought about the hour, it was after two in the morning.

The two men stood up and said they must go and sleep, because they had to be at work at half past seven. They had brought Haddouj and she left with them. Bachir shut the door and stumbled back into the room. He sat down on the divan, picked up a half-empty bottle and drank from it, looking across at Abdeslam in the corner smoking his pipe. I've waited a long time for this, he said. Come on, let's go to bed.

Now that they were alone together Abdeslam felt much more frightened. Wait, he said.

Wait for what? For you to run out on me?

I'm not going to do that, Bachir.

I know you're not, because I'm going to be right on top of you the whole time. Come on.

Drink your wine, said Abdeslam.

Bachir laughed. You want to see the bottle empty? Is that it? He drank all the wine, wiped his mouth and set the bottle on the taifor. There it is, he said. Now what do you want to see?

Abdeslam did not answer and Bachir rose to his feet. Come on, we've got work to do.

Abdeslam saw that Bachir was not going to drink any more.

Work? Now? He pretended not to understand.

This is our wedding-night. That means a lot of work. Bachir swayed and took a step forward to balance himself. The taifor was between them, at Bachir's feet, covered with bottles and glasses and plates.

Abdeslam stood up and began to walk slowly towards Bachir, looking steadily at his face. When he got to the taifor he stopped walking. Then he kicked the taifor hard, so that its edge hit Bachir on both shins.

Bachir fell forward, face-down on to the taifor, and his arm broke a glass. Abdeslam had his hand in his pocket, getting the lemon out of the handkerchief. Now he had it comfortably in his hand.

Bachir began to raise himself up slowly. He looked at the blood running down his arm. You're not going to get away tonight, he said.

Abdeslam stood still, watching Bachir as he got to his feet. His heart was beating very hard.

Bachir stepped round the taifor, threw out his arms and lunged forward. Abdeslam struck at his hand with the lemon.

Bachir cried out, bent forward and clapped his good hand over the cut one. At that moment Abdeslam brought the lemon down on Bachir's cheek. It laid the flesh open from his ear to his mouth, making two long slashes.

Bachir was bent over farther now, with his face in his hands. Abdeslam kicked him with all his might in the groin, and he doubled up and fell in a heap.

For a moment Abdeslam stood looking down at him. Then he heard Bachir's heavy breathing. He ran into his room and got his suitcase. As he came back through the middle room he saw Bachir moving on the floor with his red hands over his face. He threw the key under the sink, and remembered that he had left his train and the mechanical animals in the mahal.

The rain had stopped. He shut the door and walked down the alley. He went as far as the corner without looking back, but then he turned, to be sure that Bachir was not behind him.

The door was still shut. He shifted his suitcase to the other hand and turned the corner.

It was not long before people began to forget that his name was Abdeslam. They called him The Lemon.

CITY LIGHTS PUBLICATIONS

Angulo, Jamie de. *JAIME IN TAOS*
Antler. *FACTORY (Pocket Poets #38)*
Artaud, Antonin. *ANTHOLOGY*
Baudelaire, Charles. *INTIMATE JOURNALS*
Bowles, Paul. *A HUNDRED CAMELS IN THE COURTYARD*
Breá, Juan & Mary Low. *RED SPANISH NOTEBOOK*
Brecht, Stefan. *POEMS (Pocket Poets #36)*
Broughton, James. *SEEING THE LIGHT*
Buckley, Lord. *HIPARAMA OF THE CLASSICS*
Buhle, Paul. *FREE SPIRITS: Annals of the Insurgent Imagination*
Bukowski, Charles. *THE MOST BEAUTIFUL WOMAN IN TOWN*
Bukowski, Charles. *NOTES OF A DIRTY OLD MAN*
Bukowski, Charles. *SHAKESPEARE NEVER DID THIS*
Bukowski, Charles. *TALES OF ORDINARY MADNESS*
Burroughs, William S. *ROOSEVELT AFTER INAUGURATION*
Burroughs, William S. *THE BURROUGHS FILE*
Burroughs, W.S. & Allen Ginsberg. *THE YAGE LETTERS*
Carrington, Leonora. *THE HEARING TRUMPET*
Cassady, Neal. *THE FIRST THIRD*
Charters, Ann, ed. *SCENES ALONG THE ROAD*
CITY LIGHTS JOURNAL No. 4
Codrescu, Andrei. *IN AMERICA'S SHOES*
Corso, Gregory. *GASOLINE/VESTAL LADY ON BRATTLE (Pocket Poets #8)*
David Neel, Alexandra. *SECRET ORAL TEACHINGS IN TIBETAN BUDDHIST SECTS*
Di Prima, Diane. *REVOLUTIONARY LETTERS*
Doolittle, Hilda. *(H.D.) NOTES ON THOUGHT & VISION*
Duncan, Isadora. *ISADORA SPEAKS*
Eberhardt, Isabelle. *THE OBLIVION SEEKERS*
Fenollosa, Ernest. *THE CHINESE WRITTEN CHARACTER AS A MEDIUM FOR POETRY*
Ferlinghetti, Lawrence. *LEAVES OF LIFE*
Ferlinghetti, Lawrence. *PICTURES OF THE GONE WORLD (Pocket Poets #1)*
Ferlinghetti, Lawrence. *SEVEN DAYS IN NICARAGUA LIBRE*
Gascoyne, David. *A SHORT SURVEY OF SURREALISM*
Ginsberg, Allen. *THE FALL OF AMERICA (Pocket Poets #30)*
Ginsberg, Allen. *HOWL & OTHER POEMS (Pocket Poets #4)*
Ginsberg, Allen. *INDIAN JOURNALS*
Ginsberg, Allen. *IRON HORSE*

Ginsberg, Allen. *KADDISH & OTHER POEMS (Pocket Poets #14)*
Ginsberg, Allen. *MIND BREATHS (Pocket Poets #35)*
Ginsberg, Allen. *PLANET NEWS (Pocket Poets #23)*
Ginsberg, Allen. *PLUTONIAN ODE (Pocket Poets #40)*
Ginsberg, Allen. *REALITY SANDWICHES (Pocket Poets #18)*
Herron, Don. *THE LITERARY WORLD OF SAN FRANCISCO
& ITS ENVIRONS*
Higman, Perry, tr. *LOVE POEMS from Spain and
Spanish America*
Hirschman, Jack. *LYRIPOL (Pocket Poets #34)*
Kerouac, Jack. *BOOK OF DREAMS*
Kerouac, Jack. *SCATTERED POEMS (Pocket Poets #28)*
Kovic, Ron. *A DANGEROUS COUNTRY*
Kovic, Ron. *AROUND THE WORLD IN EIGHT DAYS*
La Duke, Betty. *COMPAÑERAS: Women, Art & Social Change
in Latin America*
Lamantia, Philip. *BECOMING VISIBLE (Pocket Poets #39)*
Lamantia, Philip. *MEADOWLARK WEST*
Lamantia, Philip. *SELECTED POEMS (Pocket Poets #20)*
Laughlin, James. *SELECTED POEMS 1935-1985*
Lowry, Malcolm. *SELECTED POEMS (Pocket Poets #17)*
Lucebert. *NINE DUTCH POETS (Pocket Poets #42)*
Ludlow, Fitzhugh. *THE HASHEESH EATER*
McDonough, Kay. *ZELDA*
Moore, Daniel. *BURNT HEART*
Mrabet, Mohammed. *M'HASHISH*
Mrabet, Mohammed. *THE LEMON*
Murguia, A. *VOLCAN: Poems from Central America*
Newton, Huey & Ericka Huggins. *INSIGHTS & POEMS*
O'Hara, Frank. *LUNCH POEMS (Pocket Poets #19)*
Olson, Charles. *CALL ME ISHMAEL*
Orlovsky, Peter. *CLEAN ASSHOLE POEMS & SMILING
VEGETABLE SONGS (Pocket Poets #37)*
Pickard, Tom. *GUTTERSNIPE*
Plymell, Charles. *THE LAST OF THE MOCCASINS*
Poe, Edgar Allan. *THE UNKNOWN POE*
Prévert, Jacques. *PAROLES (Pocket Poets #9)*
Rey Rosa, Rodrigo. *THE BEGGAR'S KNIFE*
Rigaud, Milo. *SECRETS OF VOODOO*
Rips, Geoffrey. *UNAMERICAN ACTIVITIES*
Rosemont, Franklin. *SURREALISM & ITS
POPULAR ACCOMPLICES*
Sanders, Ed. *INVESTIGATIVE POETRY*

Shepard, Sam. *FOOL FOR LOVE*
Shepard, Sam. *MOTEL CHRONICLES*
Snyder, Gary. *THE OLD WAYS*
Solomon, Carl. *MISHAPS PERHAPS*
Solomon, Carl. *MORE MISHAPS*
Waldman, Anne. *FAST SPEAKING WOMAN (Pocket Poets #33)*
Waley, Arthur. *THE NINE SONGS*
Wilson, Colin. *POETRY AND MYSTICISM*
Yevtushenko, Yevgeni. *RED CATS (Pocket Poets #16)*